Tony
Hawk

Tony Hawk

by Barbara Sheen

LUCENT BOOKS

An imprint of Thomson Gale, a part of The Thomson Corporation

Detroit • New York • San Francisco • New Haven, Conn. • Waterville, Maine • London

For more information, contact:
Lucent Books
27500 Drake Rd.
Farmington Hills, MI 48331-3535
Or you can visit our Internet site at http://www.gale.com

LIBRARY OF CONGRESS CATALOGING-IN-PUBLICATION DATA

Sheen, Barbara.
  Tony Hawk / by Barbara Sheen.
    p. cm. — (People in the news)
  Includes bibliographical references and index.
  ISBN 978-1-4205-0016-5 (hardcover)
  1. Hawk, Tony—Juvenile literature. 2. Skateboarders—United States—Biography—Juvenile literature. I. Title.
  GV859.813.H39S54 2008
  796.22092—dc22
  [B]
                                                          2007024365

ISBN-10: 1-4205-0016-3

Printed in the United States of America

Contents

ame and celebrity are alluring. People are drawn to those who
walk in fame's spotlight, whether they are known for great
accomplishments or for notorious deeds. The lives of the famous
pique public interest and attract attention, perhaps because their
experiences seem in some ways so different from, yet in other
ways so similar to, our own.

Newspapers, magazines, and television regularly capitalize
on this fascination with celebrity by running profiles of famous
people. For example, television programs such as _Entertainment
Tonight_ devote all their programming to stories about entertain-
ment and entertainers. Magazines such as _People_ fill their pages
with stories of the private lives of famous people. Even newspapers, newsmagazines, and television news frequently delve
into the lives of well-known personalities. Despite the number
of articles and programs, few provide more than a superficial
glimpse at their subjects.

Lucent's People in the News series offers young readers a
deeper look into the lives of today's newsmakers, the influences
that have shaped them, and the impact they have had in their
fields of endeavor and on other people's lives. The subjects of the
series hail from many disciplines and walks of life. They include
authors, musicians, athletes, political leaders, entertainers, entre-
preneurs, and others who have made a mark on modern life and
who, in many cases, will continue to do so for years to come.

These biographies are more than factual chronicles. Each book
emphasizes the contributions, accomplishments, or deeds that
have brought fame or notoriety to the individual and shows how
that person has influenced modern life. Authors portray their subjects in a realistic, unsentimental light. For example, Bill Gates —
the cofounder and chief executive officer of the software giant
Microsoft — has been instrumental in making personal comput-
ers the most vital tool of the modern age. Few dispute his business
savvy, his perseverance, or his technical expertise, yet critics say
he is ruthless in his dealings with competitors and driven more by

his desire to maintain Microsoft's dominance in the computer industry than by an interest in furthering technology.

In these books, young readers will encounter inspiring stories about real people who achieved success despite enormous obstacles. Oprah Winfrey — the most powerful, most watched, and wealthiest woman on television today — spent the first six years of her life in the care of her grandparents while her unwed mother sought work and a better life elsewhere. Her adolescence was colored by promiscuity, pregnancy at age fourteen, rape, and sexual abuse.

Each author documents and supports his or her work with an array of primary and secondary source quotations taken from diaries, letters, speeches, and interviews. All quotes are footnoted to show readers exactly how and where biographers derive their information and provide guidance for further research. The quotations enliven the text by giving readers eyewitness views of the life and accomplishments of each person covered in the People in the News series.

In addition, each book in the series includes photographs, annotated bibliographies, timelines, and comprehensive indexes. For both the casual reader and the student researcher, the People in the News series offers insight into the lives of today's newsmakers —people who shape the way we live, work, and play in the modern age.

Ups and Downs

Tony Hawk is the most successful and influential skate-boarder of all time. His rise to stardom, however, was not without setbacks. Both Hawk and the sport he has come to represent have had their ups and downs. In many ways, Hawk's

Skateboarding's image in the past has been negative, but that has changed. It is now a respected sport.

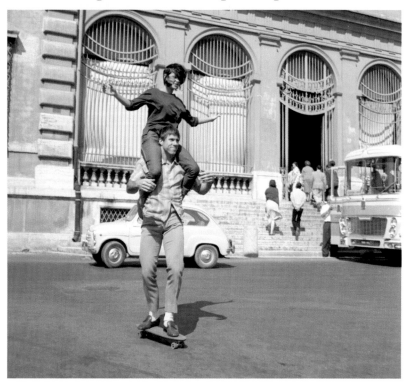

skateboarding career mirrors the growth and changes in the sport itself.

Skateboarding began in the 1960s. From that time on, the sport experienced several periods of widespread popularity as well as times when interest in skateboarding declined. In fact, there were periods when skateboarding was not considered to be a true sport or was even felt to be socially unacceptable. "I have been a professional skateboarder for twenty-four years," Hawk explained in 2006. "For most of that time, the activity that paid my rent, and gave me my greatest joy was tagged with many labels, most of which were ugly. It was a kid's fad, a waste of time, a dangerous pursuit, a crime."[1]

Skateboarding's negative image has finally changed. The sport has now become a respected part of the mainstream sporting scene. Most people think that skateboarding's widespread appeal is thanks to Tony Hawk. He, more than anyone else, has helped to make skateboarding the popular action sport it is today.

Changing Times

When Hawk started skating competitively in the early 1980s skateboarding had already reached its first peak in popularity and was on the decline. There was little public interest in the sport and, therefore, little money to be made by skateboarding. Although Hawk was already showing tremendous talent as a skateboarder, he received little recognition. Worse still, he was made to feel like a social outcast by his peers at school who believed anyone who still skated was a loser. Despite the unpopularity of the sport, his classmates' teasing, and the unlikelihood of ever making money skating, Tony did not quit. His passion for the sport was too strong. "Find the thing you love," he advises. "You might not make it to the top, but if you are doing what you love, there is much more happiness there than being rich or famous."[2]

Tony's determination paid off. As his skills and confidence grew, skateboarding experienced another revival. At the age of eighteen, Hawk had become a celebrity in the skateboarding world. He had

Hawk's advice: "Find the thing you love."

been on two world tours and had his own signature skateboard, sales of which earned him enough money to purchase a house.

Then in 1991, skateboarding once again fell out of favor and Hawk's perfect life came crashing down. After interviewing Hawk, for Teen Ink, a Web site written by and for teens, reporter David G. explained that Hawk, "talked about how his life was not always so miraculous. He mentioned one day he was skating on top of the world, and the next day the sport of skateboarding fell right on its face."[3]

Things got so bad for Hawk that he was forced to depend on his wife's small salary for financial support. "I had to scrape together gas money and regarded dinner at Taco Bell as a big night out,"[4] he recalls.

Another X-treme

Just as Hawk's career as a skateboarder hit rock bottom and he thought he would have to give up the sport he loved in order to pay his bills, skateboarding was resurrected. The introduction of the X (for extreme) Games in 1995 by the cable television sports channel, ESPN, brought skateboarding and Hawk back into the public eye on a massive scale. One hundred and ninety-eight thousand people attended the 1995 games. Millions more watched the games on television as Hawk flew through the air performing tricks that seemed to defy gravity. Almost overnight, the popularity of Hawk and the sport of skateboarding skyrocketed. Skateboarding was finally recognized as a mainstream sport and became universally accepted—as did Tony Hawk.

High profile sponsorship deals put Hawk into the limelight and earned him a lot of money. Hawk's record-making performance in the 1999 X Games sealed his fate. When Hawk performed skateboarding's first 900 (an extremely difficult trick in which the skater spins 900 degrees in the air and rotates five times), he became one of the world's most famous and respected athletes. "Think Michael Jordan. Or Wayne Gretzky. Or Tiger Woods. Hawk belongs in their class,"[5] says *Dallas Morning News* sports columnist Jean-Jacques Taylor.

ESPN's production of the X Games in 1995 was instrumental in bringing worldwide attention to skateboarding.

No Longer an Outcast

Hawk was overwhelmed with requests for public appearances and autograph signings. These events attracted mobs of fans. In fact, when Hawk visited his former middle school in 2000, he drew such a large crowd that he needed a police escort to safely exit the campus. Hawk recalls: "There was a swarm of kids outside the class door chanting my name and demanding I come out. I guess word spread throughout the school that I was there. I hung around in the classroom … while waiting for the crowd to thin out, but the kids were persistent and didn't seem to lessen in number… As we drove through the campus in the cruiser, kids ran after us banging on the windows (of a cop car!), asking for autographs and almost getting run over in the process… Years ago I was considered an outcast and a nerd in this neighborhood because I skated, and now I needed a police escort to leave it safely."[6]

Today Hawk is no longer an outcast. He is an action sports icon who runs a multimillion dollar business empire. He is also a husband, father, bestselling author, actor, filmmaker, video game star, arena sports tour producer, radio host, and humanitarian. Yet, it is his achievements as a skater of which he is most proud.

Largely because of Hawk's success, skateboarding, too, has left behind its image as an outsider's sport. "Everything has changed," Hawk explains, "and I am proud to be considered a professional skateboarder … honored to have had so many opportunities, and grateful that people have finally accepted skateboarding for its positive aspects."[7]

Chapter 1

A Perfect Match

Tony Hawk's hyperactive nature and determination to achieve made him a challenging child to raise. Although he tried to play traditional sports, he did not have the temperament for them. It was only when he began skateboarding that he found an activity that suited his nature. Skateboarding provided Tony with an outlet for his high energy and his unflagging determination.

Having His Way

Anthony Frank Hawk was born on May 12, 1968, in San Diego, California, to Frank and Nancy Hawk. He was the youngest of four children. His parents, who were in their forties when Tony was born, liked to say that his birth was a happy surprise. Tony's siblings were quite a bit older than him. Tony was closest in age to his twelve-year-old brother Steve. His sisters, Lenore, aged twenty-one, and Patricia, eighteen, were already away at college when Tony was born.

From the beginning, Tony was a challenging child who insisted on having his own way. In one of Hawk's earliest memories, he purposely threw his toys at his babysitter. He explains,

I don't know why I threw my toys at the sweet elderly babysitter who looked after me as an infant. She never took me behind the woodpile and beat me with a shaving strap. In fact, I don't remember her ever doing anything mean to me...

The thing that pulled my trigger was that she had power over me. She told me what to eat and where to sit, when to wash and decided when to exile me to Stalag 17, my baby crib. After a few months of dealing with my target practice, she quit... My general disposition didn't change once the nanny left. In fact, that was just my warm-up. I may not have thrown toys at my parents, but I definitely participated in some serious parental abuse. Even, now I can't figure out why I was such a nightmare. I was born extremely high-strung. A picture of me as a week-old infant shows my hands clenched into fists and a faint scowl on my face. I looked like I'm ready to punch the photographer.[8]

Even though he was a difficult child, Tony's parents doted upon him. "Since my parents were fairly old when I came around, they'd outgrown the strict mom-and-pop rearing and slipped into the grandparent mentality," he explains. "Mom thought everything I did was cute, and I could do no wrong in dad's eyes."[9]

Unflagging Determination

On the rare occasions when Tony's parents did not give in to his demands, he threw a temper tantrum. Early on, he learned that persistence, which at the time he expressed through unacceptable behavior, was rewarded. For example, he hated being forced to take a nap at preschool. His hyperactive nature made it almost impossible for him to lie still when he was not tired. He recalls: "I had to be running around, tapping my feet, or deeply involved in an activity or else I went bananas from boredom. I still have nightmares about trying to stay still on my sleep mat, squeezing my eyes shut as the teacher walked by checking on us."[10]

Each morning, rather than entering the building where he would be forced to nap, Tony clung to the schoolyard fence screeching and crying. After dozens of episodes like this, Tony was expelled. His determination paid off. It was a lesson that would serve him well for the rest of his life.

Being Part of a Traditional Sports Team

Tony had more energy and determination than he could manage. His family tried to help him to put these qualities to good use. At age seven, Tony's parents enrolled him in Little League baseball. Although Tony liked playing baseball, being part of a traditional sports team (or for that matter, playing competitive games with others), did not suit his temperament.

Tony's hyperactive nature made it difficult for him to take part. He was too restless to sit on the bench and wait his turn while others played. He also did not have the patience to practice drills when he had already mastered particular skills.

Tony's need to be in control, and his desire to succeed, were other obstacles. Tony became very upset with his teammates if they did not do their very best. He did not like the fact that his success depended on the performance of others, but he was even harder on himself. Tony was determined to achieve, and if he did not, his frustration was almost uncontrollable. This became clear when he played board games with his family. If Tony was not winning, he would pick up the board game and throw it across the room. On the playing field, he took his own (and his teammates') failures personally. One time he became so distressed that he flung his bat on the ground and ran off and hid in a nearby ravine. When Frank, his father, found him, Tony refused to come out until Frank bribed him with ice cream.

Following Rules

Tony's personality also made it difficult for him to follow rules. As far as Tony was concerned, if he thought a rule was silly or if it stood in the way of his goal, he ignored it. Most traditional sports and games are laden with rules. When his mother tried to teach Tony to play tennis, his inability to follow the rules and his drive to win spoiled that experience too. Instead of gently hitting the ball over the net, Tony repeatedly smacked it as hard as he could straight at his mother. After Tony had hit his mother a half dozen times, she told him that the rules of tennis did not allow players to hit each other, and if he continued to play roughly, they were going home. At that, Tony walked off the tennis court and got into the car. "What was the point of playing a game, if you didn't try to demolish your opponent?"[11] Hawk recalls thinking.

Baseball, tennis, board games, and other traditional sports were too restrictive for Tony. Following the rules, waiting around, and depending on others did not suit his character. Tony was happier when he could keep moving, when he was in control, and when his success or failure depended upon himself.

Gifted and Frustrated

Tony's high energy caused problems at school as well. As with traditional team sports, he had trouble sitting still. His behavior disrupted the classroom, causing him to be punished frequently. In an effort to get to the root of their son's problem, his parents took him to see the school psychologist, who gave him an intelligence test. Hawk remembers:

> I was really out of control. I couldn't sit still. Sitting and listening to the teacher talk about basic math made me feel like I had ants crawling all over me. I started to perform miniaerobic workouts at my desk, fidgeting nonstop. I couldn't switch off my frenzied movement. I'm surprised the teacher didn't run over and jam a wallet into my mouth. I baffled my teachers. I baffled my parents. I baffled myself. Nobody knew what was going on. I wasn't goofing off or being a poor student— I continued to maintain excellent grades... My mom thought I was somewhat bright and my movements were due to lack of stimulation. She had the school perform an IQ [intelligence] test on me. I don't remember taking the test, but I scored 144, which placed me in the "gifted" category. The teacher explained to my parents that my main problem was that I had a twelve-year-old's brain in an eight-year-old body. My brain was telling me to do things that my body couldn't do.[12]

This was partially the cause of Tony's frustration at school, in traditional team sports, and with himself. Placing him in advanced

History of skateboards

Skateboards first appeared in the 1950s in California. At the time, these skateboards were homemade devices made by surfers who wanted to practice in the streets. These early boards were made of a wooden box or plank of wood to which small metal rollerskate wheels were attached. Skateboards were sold for the first time in 1959. Between 1960 and 1963 50 million skateboards were sold.

Early skateboard decks were made of a variety of materials including plastic, fiberglass, and metal. In the 1970s, manufacturers started making the boards of laminated wood, because it was light and strong. This wood is still used today. Larry Stevenson also invented the kicktail shape around this time. This made the boards easier to do tricks on. Skateboard wheels were metal until 1972, when Frank Maceworthy invented urethane skateboard wheels. The new wheels revolutionized skateboards, making them faster and smoother to ride. Skateboards were also made wider at this time, which made them easier to stay on and maneuver.

Early skateboards had metal wheels.

classes provided him with the academic challenge he needed, and skateboarding did the rest.

An Old Blue Skateboard

When Tony was nine, his brother, Steve, was cleaning out the garage and found an old blue skateboard. The board was shorter and thinner than modern boards and had tiny wheels.

Steve was not a serious skateboarder. He had used the board to copy surfing moves. When he was growing up, surfers often used skateboards to practice their surfing techniques when the ocean was flat. They called this "sidewalk surfing." By the time Tony was nine, skateboarders had learned that they could go up and down empty backyard swimming pools and, if they gathered enough speed, they could fly into the air where they could spin and flip. This was the beginning of the type of vert [vertical] skating that made Tony famous. On that first day, however, Tony was not thinking of doing tricks. It took all of his effort to stand on the board and push off while maintaining his balance. Being Tony, as soon as he achieved that, he wanted to do more. He became upset by his inability to turn the board, repeatedly slamming into fences and walls in an effort to successfully maneuver it. Steve spent the remainder of the day instructing Tony on how to turn properly. Tony did not give up until he mastered the skill.

Even though Tony enjoyed skating that day, he did not take the experience seriously. At first he pulled out the board whenever he was bored, as he did with other toys such as a Frisbee or a basketball. But as time passed, Tony turned to skateboarding more often.

Oasis Skate Park

As Tony dedicated more time to skateboarding, his skills improved and his interest in the sport increased. However, Tony's only experience of skating was on the street. He lacked the facilities that would help him to do high-flying tricks. The nearest skatepark was Oasis Skate Park, which was located beneath a nearby freeway overpass. Tony had seen the park from afar whenever his family drove over it. The sight always fascinated him. He recalls:

> I'd peer out the window every time we drove over. The place always seemed to be packed. It was a few acres of gray concrete, polka-dotted with off-white pools. There were two big pools: a snake run, which is a long twisted series of hips and banks that resemble a snake; a reservoir, a halfpipe with no flatbottom; and a flat beginner's area.

The frenzied activity of the hundreds of skateboarders hypnotized me. They looked like molecules in the middle of a nuclear reaction. Skateboarders whipped by in every direction, carving the bowls and popping tiny airs and inverts. I was surprised they never hit each other. I nagged my parents, moaning like a dying man about how badly I needed an Oasis membership."[13]

This was one of the few times, however, that Tony's parents refused him. Tony's father suffered a heart attack shortly before Tony was born. When Frank was able to return to work, his position had been filled. From that time on, Frank experienced periods when he was unemployed. This was one of those times. Money, therefore, was scarce in the Hawk household and skatepark fees

Oasis Skate Park was the first facility Tony ever skated on.

were not in the family's budget. However, to satisfy Tony, Frank built a small skating ramp in the driveway. The homemade ramp did not compare with what Oasis had to offer, but Tony made do with it for the next year.

When he was in fifth grade, Tony's friend's mother volunteered to take a group of neighborhood boys to Oasis. Tony once again pleaded with his parents to let him go. Because Frank was now working, they agreed.

From the moment that Tony walked through the park's gates, he was spellbound. All the skaters moving at breakneck speeds doing seemingly impossible tricks amazed and inspired him. Tony decided that one day he would be one of those daredevils. He was hooked on the thrills of skating and the challenges of learning and perfecting new tricks. From that day on, skating became Tony's main focus. "For the first time I was feeling content, "Tony recalls. "Even though I wasn't close to being a good skater, I felt happy thinking about the possibilities skating had to offer. I wasn't frustrated or discouraged… I couldn't wait to go back again. From that day on my life changed."[14]

A Different Boy

Tony began spending all his spare time at Oasis. To pay for his new hobby, he got a job delivering newspapers. He used the money he earned to pay for a park pass and new skating equipment.

Tony's family soon noticed a change in the boy. He finally had an outlet for his energy and determination. Unlike traditional team sports, skateboarding suited him. There were no practice schedules, coaches, or other players that Tony had to wait for or rely on. What he achieved depended solely on his own efforts. He was finally in charge. The pleasure and freedom that Tony got from skating and the pride he felt when he mastered a new trick had a positive effect on him. He was calmer, happier, and more pleasant to be around. "Skating changed his personality," explains Tony's brother. "Finally, he was doing something that he was satisfied with."[15]

When he found skateboarding, Tony found himself. (Shown here with his father, Frank.)

Talent and Skills

Tony worked very hard in an effort to improve as a skater. He sought out older, more experienced skaters to help him. Dave Andrecht, a famous skateboarder from the 1970s, took Tony under his wing. When Dave was unavailable, Tony studied the

Skateboarding Vocabulary

Skateboarders seem to have a language all of their own. Here are some common skateboarding terms and their meaning.

air: Riding the skateboard in the air.
bail: To jump off the board or fall purposefully to avoid crashing.
backside: Facing away from the ramp while doing a stunt.
coping: Metal pipe running along the edge of a skateboard ramp.
deck: The body of the skateboard on which the skater stands.
demo: Skating exhibition.
fakie: Skating backwards.
frontside: Facing the ramp while doing a stunt.
grab: Clutching the skateboard with the hands while in the air.
grind: To scrape the truck of a skateboard on a curb or coping.
halfpipe: A U-shaped ramp with high sides.
kickflip: Spinning the board after ollieing.
nose: The front of the skateboard.
ollie: To pop the tail of the board up in order to become airborne.
shoveit: To turn the skateboard without turning the body, so that the board spins under the skater's feet.
slam: To crash or fall.
tail: The rear of the skateboard.
truck: Two axles that attach the skateboard wheels to the deck.
vert: A form of skateboarding that uses a ramp to launch the skater into the air.

The halfpipe is a place where skaters can perform high-flying tricks.

more experienced skaters and copied their moves. He spent hours trying to master new tricks and refused to leave the park until he was satisfied with his own performance. This was often difficult for Tony's father, who drove Tony to and from Oasis everyday. One day, for example, Tony was trying to learn a difficult trick in which the skater flips upside down in the air, and he made his father wait for hours. Tony insisted that if he could just try the trick five hundred more times he would have it!

In spite of Tony's driven nature, his parents gave him tremendous support. They did everything they could to help Tony, sharing his love of skating and encouraging him to succeed. His father, in particular, devoted much of his own life to Tony's skateboarding career, something that Tony will be forever grateful for.

The time and effort Tony put into skateboarding were beginning to pay off. His skating skills improved on a daily basis. Within a short time, he was excelling at basic skateboarding tricks like grinds (a maneuver in which the skater rides along obstacles like the edge of the skatepark deck or a curb) and was attempting even more challenging tricks. At the age of eleven, Tony began to enter competitions. He had found his passion.

Chapter 2

Developing a
New Style

As Tony's enthusiasm for skating increased, the sport's popularity fell. Skateboarding became unfashionable and many skaters chose to give it up. But Tony never wavered in his passion for skateboarding. And soon he developed a new style of skating that would change the sport forever.

On the Decline

Skateboarding had been very popular during the 1960s and 1970s. However, by 1980, shortly after Tony began skating competitively, the sport's popularity began to decline. BMX biking replaced skateboarding in popularity. Lack of attendance and rising insurance costs forced skateparks to close down. However, Tony remained dedicated to the sport. He explains:

> I seemed to have an adverse effect on skating, because the more I liked it the less popular it became. The early 1980s were the black plague of skateboarding. It was as if every skate park had a black X painted on its door. The booming business, with millions of participants, died almost overnight and no one seemed to know why. Skaters dropped out of the scene with impressive indifference. One day I'd skate with a park buddy and the next week he would be gone, never to be seen again. The dozens of nearby parks

toppled like a stack of dominoes, ASPO [the Association of Skate Park Owners, an organization that promoted skateboard competitions] limped around ready to die, and I was more hyped on skating than ever.[16]

A Nonconformist

At a time when other people his age tried hard to fit in, Tony's passion for skateboarding made him an outsider. Tony began high school in eighth grade and at twelve years old, he looked much younger than his actual age. He was short and skinny, weighing 80 pounds (36.29kg) and measuring under 5 feet (1.52m). Tony's size, his obsession with what was thought to be a loser's sport, his strange skater's wardrobe, and his scraped knees and ankles made him an outcast who was teased and bullied. "I was considered a loser geek who still participated in a silly "fad" that everyone knew was out. I had no friends at school,"[17] Hawk explains.

Even some of Tony's teachers gave him a hard time. They made it obvious that they were not impressed with skateboarding. Tony recounts one incident, "The teacher said I'd never make a living as a skateboarder, so it seemed to *him* that my future was bleak."[18]

It would have been easier for Tony to stop skating and to try to blend in. But he never wavered in his devotion to skating. "You've got to follow your heart," he insists, "and not worry about what other people are saying."[19] In so doing, Tony developed as a skater, inventing new tricks and a new skating style that would make Tony famous and revolutionize skateboarding forever.

Not Enough Power

Although the skatepark was a place where Tony could escape from the nightmare he faced at school, his life as a skater was not problem-free. Tony's small size made it more difficult for him to skate. Before skaters can do the flips and spins known as aerials or airs, they need to jump into the air. To do this, they

Ollieing is a technique Tony learned early in order to compensate for his slight physique.

need a lot of power and speed to grab their boards and launch themselves at least six feet (1.83m) into the air. Skaters with more muscle and body mass have an advantage. Hawk jokingly refers to his youthful physique as that of a noodle. When Tony grabbed his board, his light weight slowed him down and he could not get into the air. Instead, Tony learned a technique called an ollie.

The ollie was invented in the late 1970s by a thirteen-year-old skater named Alan "Ollie" Gelfand. To perform an ollie, skaters lift their boards up with their back foot while keeping it stable with their front foot. This helps the skater to become airborne without losing the board. When Tony learned to ollie, the trick was unpopular. However, Tony had no choice; if he did not perform the trick, he would remain on the ground.

Types of Skateboarding

There are many different types of skateboarding. When Hawk started skating, the most popular style was freestyle. Freestyle skating, which is rarely done today, is graceful skating similar to dancing. It is often done to music.

Slalom and downhill skating are similar to skiing. Both are done on a straight downhill ramp that imitates a ski slope. In slalom, the skater maneuvers between obstacles, while in downhill the skater skates downhill very fast. This is usually done on a long board.

Street skating is done on streets. Skaters ollie off obstacles such as curbs or benches. Cruising is a form of street skating in which skaters use their skateboards as a means of transportation. Offroad skating takes skaters off the streets and onto dirt. It uses special large boards with very big wheels. The skaters feet are strapped onto the board.

Vert skating is done in skateparks on long ramps called halfpipes. Vert skaters do high-flying tricks.

Unfortunately for Tony, most skaters at the time thought that the ollie was a form of cheating. Many skaters looked down on Tony for doing the trick. However, the technique soon became the foundation for most of Tony's moves. He remembers:

> I weighed slightly more than a Chihuahua—this fact... being my largest obstacle in skateboarding at the time. I was so light I couldn't produce enough momentum to do most tricks, so I learned a different technique to pop higher; I ollied into my airs. At the time, my style was a huge joke; nobody ollied into tricks, everybody early grabbed. My "cheating" style would be mocked for the next five years, but I had no choice. It was either ollie or stop progressing. It wasn't a logical innovation for me; it was simply an unfortunate (or so I thought at the time) solution to my problem.[20]

No one could have predicted that future generations of skaters would copy Hawk's use of the ollie, making the manuever the basis for almost every move in modern vert skating. According to Tony, "The ollie... has become an essential part of every serious skateboarder's repertoire—the equivalent of a plié for a ballet dancer... It is the skateboarder's way of expressing his desire to fly."[21]

The Robotic Circus Skater

Ollieing was not the only way that made Tony's skating stand out. Tony's lack of muscle prohibited him from having the smooth skating style that was popular at the time. While other skaters seemed to glide effortlessly, in order to skate a half-pipe (a U-shaped ramp with walls that can be 15 feet (4.5m) high), Tony pumped his legs like he was on a swing. He bent his knees as he skated down the skateboard ramp and then, as he reached the other end of the ramp, he stood up. By pushing his weight upward, he gained enough force to reach the top of the ramp, which was otherwise difficult for a skater of his size. Pumping made Tony look stiff and strange. According to the other skaters, Tony had the style of a robot. An article on Outside Online, a Web site dedicated to action sports, puts it this way: "In the early days,

Tony was considerably handicapped by his pipe-stem physique." "People did not take him seriously at first, because he looked like a puppet," recalls Stacy Peralta, 45, a famous skateboarder and promoter... "He was so fine-boned and brittle-looking, we thought, if he ever falls he's going to break like porcelain."

"The guy was just a stick man," agrees Grant Brittain, the photo editor of Trans-world Skateboarding magazine. Brittain, 47, ran the Del Mar Skate Ranch when Tony first started skating there in 1981. "People ... made fun of him because his skating wasn't very cool," says Brittain. "It wasn't surfer's style, and getting that fluid style was all that mattered back then." [22]

To make matters worse, Tony could not master tricks that required a lot of upper body strength. To make up for this, he developed a number of new tricks in which he used alternative skating methods. In one, the finger flip air, Tony grabbed the nose of his skateboard and spun around in a half circle. Tony's unique tricks did not go down very well with some of the older skaters. They believed that Tony was not taking the sport seriously and called him a "Circus Skater." Although these comments hurt Tony, in order to progress as a skater he had to skate his own way. Tony did not have the body type to do otherwise. As a result, he continued to develop new tricks and create a skating style that ultimately took over the sport.

Competing

Despite the many new tricks Tony invented, his first competition was not successful. He was so anxious on the way to the skatepark that he almost made himself sick. During the drive, Tony obsessively went over his skating routine in his mind. Each time he did, he saw new ways that he could fail. By the time he reached the park, Tony was a bundle of nerves. He seriously thought about asking his parents to take him home, but his strong determination kept him there.

Tony's performance at the competition matched his worst expectations. Because he was so scared, he messed up on tricks that he could perform perfectly in practice. However,

Skateboarding Safety

Skateboarding accidents send an estimated 26,000 people to hospital emergency rooms in the United States each year. Wearing proper safety equipment can help protect skaters from serious injuries, which is why Tony Hawk never attempts a skateboarding trick without such equipment.

A helmet is the most important safety item. Wearing a helmet can protect against serious or even fatal head injuries. Skateboarding helmets have a chin-strap that should be fastened at all times. It is also essential that the helmet fits securely. The front of the helmet should come down over the skater's head to just above the eyebrows.

Knee and elbow pads are also helpful to protect the joints. Wrist braces and skating gloves protect the hands. Special padded skating shorts can be worn under the skater's pants or shorts. They provide extra cushioning if the skater falls.

Even with proper equipment, slamming is inevitable. That is why it is important for skaters to learn how to fall. Relaxing the body during a fall, trying to land on a fleshy part of the body, and rolling with a fall all help protect the skater against serious injuries.

Because of the great potential for injury, protective safety gear is very important.

although Tony did not do well in the contest, he did not surrender to his fears and he did not quit. That day was just the beginning.

Tony was soon competing a few weekends a month. To help calm his nerves, he spent hours practicing in the skateparks where each competition was held. At home, he drew a map of the skatepark. Then he listed all his tricks, carefully planning what order he would do them in. Tony made sure one trick logically followed the next, making it unnecessary for him to stop or slow down during his performance. He next drew an X on the map to indicate where each trick would start and end. Then, every night for at least a week, he pictured his run in his mind in an effort to commit it to memory.

The Perfectionist

As a result of Tony's careful preparation and constant persistence, he started doing better in competitions. But if Tony did not feel he gave his best performance, even winning was not enough to satisfy him. Tony's father, who never missed a competition, could never tell how well his son had done by his mood. Tony's actions, on the other hand, were a better indicator. If Tony was dissatisfied with his performance, he refused to talk to anyone. Instead, he shut himself in his room analyzing what he had done wrong. His only company was Zorro, a black and white stray cat that Tony had rescued. "It never really mattered to me if I won, but whether I skated up to my expectations... I obsessed about my mistakes and withdrew into myself. I'd sit silently the entire drive home, walk through the door, pick up Zorro and retreat to my room. I'd lie in bed petting Zorro, trying to come to terms with my self-loathing."[23] he explains.

Tony's single-mindedness won him a place on Dogtown's skateboarding team (a skateboard manufacturer). Unlike a traditional sports team, a skateboarding team is a group of individuals who represent a skateboard manufacturer. Members of the team do not skate together or depend on each other in

If he didn't perform as well as he thought he should have, Tony shut himself in his room.

any way. In competitions each skater is scored based on his or her own performance. Skateboard teams do not win or lose competitions; individuals do. But manufacturers recruit skaters in the hope that they will become known in the skating world. Team members are given the manufacturer's products for free as a type of advertising. The manufacturer also pays the competition entry fees for each team member.

At the same time that Dogtown recruited Tony, Frank Hawk started the California Amateur Skateboard League (CASL). This league would provide plenty of organized competitions for teams like Dogtown to take part in.

Powell Peralta

Tony did not skate for Dogtown long before the company went out of business because of skateboarding's decline in popularity. But although Tony was unaware of it, a famous skateboarder named Stacy Peralta had been following his progress as a skater. Peralta was an original member of the Z-boys, one of the earliest and most famous skateboarding teams of all time. Peralta was a celebrated skateboarder in the 1970s, winning the world championship in 1977. When he retired from skating because of injuries, he got together with his friend George Powell and started a skateboard company called Powell Peralta (or Powell for short). It was the most successful skateboard company at the time, mainly because of the Bones Brigade, the company's skating team. Peralta got the world's most exciting skateboarders to represent the company. In 1980, just before Tony's thirteenth birthday, Peralta offered Tony a place on the team. While Tony had not yet reached his full potential as a skater, Peralta believed he had talent. He said that it was Tony's ability to make up new tricks and his strong determination that caught his eye.

At the same time, another well-known skateboard company, G&S, tried to attract Tony. In fact, they had already given him free equipment. Tony's father explained to him that it was not right to let each company think he was going to skate for them.

Stacy Peralta saw the potential in young Tony.

Tony had to make a choice. Whichever it was, his father would support it.

Tony chose Powell Peralta. He became the youngest member of a team that would be part of his life for the next thirteen years. Tony admits, "It was a decision that would affect my entire life in ways I couldn't understand at the time. Next to my parents, Peralta was my biggest supporter. He was one of the most positive influences in my life. He encouraged and helped to direct my skating in ways I'd never thought possible."[24]

Skating with the Bones Brigade was a challenge. Tony was now skating in national competitions in unfamiliar parks against experienced skaters from all over the country. He did not do well at first, but with the support of his teammates and Peralta's coaching, Tony's confidence and skills increased rapidly. By 1982, Tony was dominating most of the competitions he entered. These contests, however, were strictly for amateurs.

A Professional

Most of the best skaters at the time, including the other members of the Bones Brigade, were professionals. Tony's skills were now much better than other amateur competitors. Peralta felt that Tony needed the challenge of competing against professional skaters and encouraged him to become a professional. At the time, there was little difference between professional (pro) and amateur skaters. Today, pro skateboarders can win $20,000 in a contest. But back then professional skaters did well if they won $150. Skating was not a career option at the time.

Tony did not care about the income he might get as a professional. He was too young to have long-term career goals and had few expenses. He did not drive, he lived at home, and he had no social life other than skating. All that concerned him was becoming a better skater. Peralta felt that turning pro would help Tony to do this. So, in 1982, on an entry form for a contest in Whittier, California, fourteen-year-old Tony checked the professional box. He won third place in that competition, his first as a professional. When Tony told his parents that he was now a professional skateboarder, they paid little interest. They did not believe that his decision would be the start of a lifelong career. No one could have predicted what the future held for Tony.

Chapter 3

Riding the Wave

In his early years as a professional skateboarder, Tony did not earn very much money. But he was quickly becoming well known in the skateboarding world, winning competitions and inventing new tricks. As Tony's popularity rose, so too did the popularity of the sport he loved. As a result, Tony's earnings skyrocketed.

A World Traveler

By 1983, Tony was becoming a celebrity in the skateboarding community. In fact, he had already appeared on the cover of *Thrasher* magazine, a new skateboarding publication. That summer he performed with the Bones Brigade on an international skating tour. Although the tour did not attract huge crowds, the number of people in the audience was on the rise.

Tony's gravity-defying tricks and his unique skating style did not go unnoticed by skateboarding fans. Increasingly, autograph collectors sought him out. Other skaters were also taking notice. The technique of ollieing was becoming accepted, and many skaters were trying to do the airborne twists, flips, and spins that Tony was becoming known for. Among his newest and most imitated tricks were the airwalk and the gymnast plant. In the first, Tony grabbed the board with one hand while splitting his legs open as if he was walking on air. The second trick was a one-handed handstand. To do it, Tony held the board in the air with one hand while he grabbed the edge of the half-pipe with the other. His feet never touched the ground.

Tony continued to develop new gravity-defying tricks.

The Screaming Chicken Skull

With skateboarding and Tony's popularity rising, Powell Peralta decided to manufacture a Tony Hawk skateboard. Other than prize money, the only way that skaters could earn money was by putting their names on items such as skateboards. Each time the item sold, the skater received a royalty (a small percentage of the profit).

Each skater's board had its own logo, which in some way represented him or her. For his logo, Tony asked one of his friends to draw a picture of a hawk swooping down on its prey. Neither Tony nor his friend was a professional artist, and the design was not very successful. Tony often jokes that the board was the worst-selling skateboard in history. Indeed, Tony's first royalty check was for 85 cents—which meant that only one person in the world bought the board!

Tony Hawk, Celebrity

Hawk's success as a skateboarder opened many doors to him. During his career he has appeared in a number of motion pictures, including *Thrasher, Gleaming the Cube, Duelin Firemen, Police Academy 4, The New Guy,* and the Imax film, *Ultimate X.*

Hawk has also made frequent television appearances. In fact, he created and appeared in the series, *ESPN's Gigantic Skate Park Tour.* He has also been featured on such shows as *Celebrity Poker, Late Night with David Letterman, The Tonight Show, Mad TV, CSI: Miami, Jimmy Kimmel Live, Punk'd,* and *The Today Show,* to name a few. On *The Today Show,* he ollied over commentator Ann Curry. Hawk has also played the voice of his own character on *The Simpsons.*

Hawk provided the voice of his own character on The Simpsons.

Hawk and his 5,000-square-foot home were featured on *MTV's Cribs.* He was also a presenter at the Billboard Music Awards, as well as being a presenter and winner at the Nickelodeon Kid's Choice Awards and the Teen Choice Awards.

It only took a few months for Powell Peralta to stop selling the board and replace it with a new design. This time, the design was created by a graphic artist and featured a hawk skull and an iron cross. Tony liked it immediately and nicknamed it "The Screaming Chicken Skull". The public was equally enthusiastic. Sales of the board took off and Tony was earning as much as $1,000 a month in royalties. Hawk says, "That was serious cash for a fifteen-year-old. I thought I won the lottery." [25] As a matter of fact, the Screaming Chicken Skull turned out to be one of the most popular selling skateboards of all time.

Video Star

In 1983, a few months after the Screaming Chicken Skull hit the market, Powell Peralta released the *Bones Brigade Video Show*. Featuring the brigade members performing their most difficult tricks, the video gave the public a chance to experience firsthand the exhilaration and freedom of skateboarding. Timed to hit the market just as VCRs were becoming a common household accessory, the video was a huge success and quickly became a favorite among skaters throughout the world. By raising the profile of the skaters who appeared in the video, the sales of the Brigade members' skateboards also increased considerably. Tony was now earning about $3,000 a month in board royalties.

The video also served a wider purpose. It changed the public's growing interest in skateboarding into a skateboarding boom. Skateboarding once again became the hot new craze. Young people all over the world were taking up the sport.

A Controversial Winner

Tony's skills had made him very famous but his newfound success was not without controversy. Before 1983, there was no organization supervising professional skateboarding competitions. In order to bring structure to the sport, Tony's father started the National Skateboarding Association (NSA). Although almost everyone in the skateboarding world approved of the association, some skaters complained that having Tony's father as the organizer presented a conflict of interests. They suggested that Frank started the organization simply to boost his son's career. Hawk describes what happened:

> I will be the first to admit that I wouldn't have been this successful without the enthusiastic support of my parents, but I'd be lying if I claimed that it didn't cause problems when I was growing up. After my dad had helped get the CASL up and running, he turned his attention to the professional skateboard contest circuit. At the time, pro contests weren't

unified and there was no ranking system. So, in 1983, he started the National Skateboarding Association (NSA) to fix some of the problems. Skaters and people involved in the industry appreciated what my dad was doing, but I felt the pressure right away. I was a relatively new pro, and my dad was running the official contest series… People started whispering the contests might be fixed in my favor.[26]

In reality, Tony's father had no ulterior motives. He would never have thought of manipulating a contest in Tony's or anyone's favor. He also had nothing to do with judging the contestants. Tony's wins were based strictly on the quality of his performance.

Nevertheless, Frank's presence put Tony in an awkward position. Fortunately, the other skaters eventually came to realize that Frank was not influencing the competition results. Most, in fact, developed long-lasting affection for the man. As for Tony, his love for his father was far stronger than any discomfort his father's presence caused him. Indeed, in the future he would link much of his success to his father's extraordinary support.

World Champion

In the first few months that Tony skated under the NSA, his competition results were mixed. He did well in parks he was familiar with but was less successful on unfamiliar ground. These failures were partly because of lack of confidence, as well as Tony's inexperience. He says, "I bounced all over the results. Sometimes I won and skated the best I could, and sometimes I couldn't stay on my board if I was Krazy Glued to it. I needed to learn to skate consistently no matter what park it was."[27]

Performing in demos (skating exhibitions) in skateparks throughout the United States with the Bones Brigade helped Tony to learn to skate in different venues. He was very pleased when he won a competition in St. Petersburg, Florida, his first win in an unfamiliar skate park. That win helped boost Tony's confidence. By the end of 1983, Tony had won three competitions, placed fourth in two, and sixth in another. Under the NSA's guidelines, skaters earned points for their rankings in competitions. At the year's end, the skater with the most points was named the National Skateboarding Association's World Champion. In 1983, the champion was Tony.

This title, however, held little meaning for Tony. His main concern was achieving his personal best. Tony, according to former Bones Brigade member Rodney Mullen, "was never satisfied with himself. He's got this nagging for perfection. It has nothing to do with the money or external praise... It's something inside himself—a duty he feels to his gifts." [28]

More Wins

Over the next two years, Tony came closer and closer to meeting his personal goals, one of which was to master a 540 McTwist. This trick, which was invented by skater Mike McGill, is one of the most difficult skating maneuvers to perfect. It features one and a half rotations with a flip in the middle. It took Tony two months of constant practice to learn the trick. At first, all his attempts were failures. But he was sure that he could do it and never gave up. "I wasn't a fast learner," Hawk explains. "But I refused to give up once I decided to try something. There were many days that I left the skate park frustrated, but I knew that I would return and figure out what I was doing wrong." [29]

Tony was not alone in trying to learn the 540 McTwist. Every vert skater was equally determined. Mastery of the technique singled out the good skaters. Performing the trick became an unspoken requirement for winning competitions. Tony started to regularly include the 540 in all his routines. Indeed, he became so fond of the trick that years later he would stun viewers by performing four in a row. Not surprisingly, Tony once again won the NSA world championship in 1984 and 1985.

Other good things were also happening in Tony's life. In 1983, at the start of his sophomore year, Tony moved to Torrey Pines High School. This school was more supportive of its nonconformist students. Tony had recently bleached parts of his hair platinum blonde and he had a punk hairstyle that would soon be copied by other skaters. The informal atmosphere at his new school kept him from being bullied because he looked different. Tony also experienced a growth spurt at this time. Although he was still very thin, he was now more than 6 feet (1.83m) tall. His added height gave him more power as a skater. If he had started skating at this time, he might have been able to achieve the fluid style of his peers. But it was impossible for him to change his skating style at this point. Instead, he concentrated on inventing new tricks. He explains:

> A lot of people still made fun of my style. I hated it and would have changed it if I could have. To hear fellow pro-skaters ripping on it behind my back made me even more bummed. My friends Chris Miller and Christian Hosoi didn't do as many tricks as I did, but they had the best styles in skateboarding. They looked super smooth when they skated, almost as if they were surfing the ramp instead of skating it. Everybody loved watching them skate. I tried changing my style, but the way you skate is the hardest thing to change. It can evolve as you grow, but to ask your body to relearn how to look when you're skating is impossible. Because I couldn't change that, I concentrated on the things I could change, such as inventing new tricks.[30]

Two of Tony's new tricks were the 720 (in which he rotated 720 degrees in the air doing four flips), and the Saran Wrap (a stunt in which Tony took his front foot off the front of the board and wrapped it around the nose of board while soaring in mid-air). Tony did some of his new tricks in the second Bones Brigade video, *Future Primitive*. His performance in the film was so amazing that Peralta took him aside and told him that he had the talent to win any competition he wanted in the future. Peralta was not the only one who noticed the way Tony seemed to defy gravity. *Future Primitive* was a huge success and increased Hawk's fan base considerably.

Making Money

As Tony's fame grew, so did the demands on his time. He spent almost all of his free time performing in demos and contests all over the world. Tony's hectic schedule forced him to miss a lot of school. Although it would have been easy to drop out of school, he did not consider it. Instead, he spent his spare time catching up on his studies.

By Tony's senior year, skating had become so popular that millions of people had taken up the sport and Tony was their hero. As a result, Tony's income soared. Shortly before graduation, he bought a four-bedroom house not far from his parents' home and filled it with the electronic gadgets and video games he adored. The house became a hangout for Tony's skateboarding friends. But although Tony enjoyed his new-found freedom, he did not let the good times interfere with his dedication to skating.

Retired

Tony won the world championship for the fourth straight year in 1986. He also appeared as an extra in *Thrasher*, a feature film about skateboarding gangs, and he performed in the third Bones Brigade video, *The Search for Animal Chin*.

By this time, Tony was winning almost every competition he entered, including contests in Japan where prize money often reached $10,000. Skateboarding had become so big that skate-boarders were now offered valuable sponsorship deals. Tony's face was everywhere. On the surface, his life appeared to be perfect. But Tony was not happy. The strain of being a high-profile athlete was taking its toll. The judges came to expect more of him than from the other competitors, as did the media and the fans. The pressure to keep winning was overwhelming. If Tony took second place, he was treated like a failure. In the past, competing encouraged Tony to develop new tricks and to progress as a skater. But now, his primary focus was winning. It was not what he wanted. Tony needed to take a break from competitive skating. But first he had to discuss his intentions with Peralta, since Powell Peralta stood to lose a lot of money if Tony quit competing.

Despite this, Peralta was sympathetic. He cared more about Tony than the bottom line. He told Tony,

> Taking a break, reflecting and observing and not taking on any more duties should help cool you off as well as restimulate you. You've been in a pressure cooker too long.

> There is a reason no one has matched your contest record and I think you are beginning to understand why. It takes a person with much inner strength to accomplish what you have. But, at the same time, accomplishing this much can be overwhelming and demanding. Sustaining the intensity which is required can wear you out.

> Tony, I have a great deal of belief in you and I will stand by whatever decision you make. From my experience, I can see what you are going through as a natural stage of your career, not an easy one at all, but a necessary one. It is time to take stock and reevaluate.[31]

During his career, Hawk has invented more than 80 tricks.

Tony's Tricks

Tony Hawk invented more than eighty tricks during his career. The following is a list of some of his tricks. It is taken from TonyHawk.com, the skater's official Web site.

1980 – backside varial
1981 – shove-it rock 'n roll, fakie-to-frontside rock, ollie-to-indy
1982 – fingerflip backside air, gay twist
1983 – frontside 540 rodeo flip, lipside reverse
1984 – airwalk-to-fakie, Madonna
1985 – stale fish, 720
1986 – backside-ollie-to-tail, indy 540
1987 – frontside gay twist, nose grind, 360 frontside rock 'n roll
1988 – frontside cab, stale fish 540, eggplant-to-fakie
1989 – ollie 540, backside rewind grind, frontside hurricane-to-fakie
1990 – frontside body varial revert, backside varial revert
1991 – cab-to-tail, 360 varial disaster, tail grab one-footed 540
1992 – heelflip varial lien, frontside noseslide
1993 – switch indy air, switch backside ollie
1994 – kickflip Mctwist, switch nollie heelflip indy
1995 – cab lipslide, cab body varial heelflip lien
1996 – switch 540, cab-to-backside Smith
1997 – frontside cab revert
1998 – varial 720, heelflip slob air, stale fish 720
1999 – 900, frontside gay twist Madonna
2000 – 360 ollie-to-backside boardslide
2001 – shove-it-to-backside Smith, frontside gay twist body varial
2002 – 360 varial Mctwist, shove-it-to-fakie frontside 5-0
2003 – 360 shove-it nose grind
2004 – shove-it fakie feeble grind

With Peralta's blessing, Tony Hawk retired from professional skateboarding in 1987. Those closest to him, however, thought his withdrawal from competitions would not be permanent.

Chapter 4

Barely Getting By

Even when he was not skating professionally, Hawk's dedication to the sport did not weaken. Skateboarding's popularity, however, was beginning to diminish and this presented Hawk with some of the greatest challenges of his career.

A Brief Retirement

Although Hawk was still performing in demos and had small roles in two major motion pictures, *Gleaming the Cube* and *Police Academy 4*, he was no longer skating competitively. This gave him time to sort out his personal life. He bought a second home about forty minutes from San Diego in Fallbrook, California, and asked his girlfriend, Cindy Dunbar, to move in with him.

The couple's new home sat on four acres of desert land. The open space around the house allowed Hawk to realize one of his lifelong dreams: having his own mini-skatepark. He explains: "The main reason I bought the property was to build ramps in my yard. Near my house I wanted a seven-foot-high [2.13m] mini-ramp with a spine. Atop the hill that crested my property, I wanted a forty-foot-wide [12.19m], twelve-and-a-half-foot-high [3.81m] spine ramp that connected with a seven-foot-deep [2.13m] bowl."[32]

Although Hawk loved skating in his private park, it did not provide him with the thrills and stimulation of competition. In 1988, he came out of retirement. But this time he was competing because he wanted to and was less focused just on winning. The change seemed to reinvigorate his skating.

Hawk bought a home in Fallbrook and built a mini-skate park on the property.

Big Changes on the Horizon

The skateboarding world welcomed Hawk's return, and he experienced great success during the late 1980s. Every demonstration and competition that he entered attracted thousands of skateboarders, who, according to sports writer Matt Christopher, came to see

> Hawk do things they had only dreamed were possible. He seemed to defy gravity as he launched himself into an Ollie an incredible six or eight feet [1.83 or 2.44m] into the air

Hawk made a series of tricks seem easy and effortless.

above the halfpipe. This provided enough height to allow him to perform an unbelievable variety of maneuvers in seemingly endless combinations. He sometimes twisted either to his frontside or backside, while other times he'd spin horizontally a full 360 or 540 degrees. Other times he turned somersaults, referred to in skateboarding as flips, grabbing the board with one hand... Then as gravity took hold and brought him back to earth, he would land the board squarely on the uppermost portion of the halfpipe, pointing at a ninety-degree angle to the ground. He would rocket down at full speed either forward or backward to the other side of the pipe and launch himself in the air again to perform another trick. Hawk was able to string these tricks together flawlessly and make it look almost effortless.[33]

Despite Hawk's incredible performances and skateboarding's increasing popularity, changes were on the horizon for both the sport and Hawk. A new way of skateboarding was beginning to take hold. It combined the daring tricks of vert skating with street skating. Rather then using the ramps found in skateparks, street skaters launched themselves into the air by ollieing off walkways, concrete stairs, benches, handrails, and curbs.

The new form of skating began as a way for skaters to avoid paying skatepark fees, but it quickly became popular with young people. Largely because of the danger the skaters posed to pedestrians, nonskaters frowned upon street skating. This was part of the sport's attraction. Street skaters considered themselves outlaws. They rejected the celebrity status of vert skaters like Hawk, labeling them sellouts. Not surprisingly, there was a growing divisiveness between the two groups. "Skating," Hawk recalls, "began to resemble high school (which is ironic, because many skaters hated high school and felt like misfits), with little cliques that didn't associate with the other, "lesser" skaters."[34]

Street skaters also took delight in the wildness of their sport. Many refused to wear safety gear and prided themselves on skating in forbidden places. Street skating, they claimed, was what skateboarding should be: risky, socially unacceptable, and raw.

Many vert skaters, including Hawk, also street skated. As a matter of fact, Hawk would win a number of street skating competitions in the future. But he never developed a passion for the sport. His attitude towards skating was different from that of hardcore street skaters. Although Hawk was not afraid of taking risks and had the scars to prove it, the recklessness of street skating did not make sense to him. "Skaters want to know how many steps you can jump. But you can only jump so far before you break a leg, even if you land it. It's getting to the point where there is no room for error. Skating isn't about danger, it's about doing things that are progressive and athletic,"[35] he insists.

Risk, rebellion, and danger were part of the growing popularity of street skating.

Despite what vert skaters thought, street skating was quickly becoming the next big craze. Companies like Powell Peralta could not compete with newer, smaller skateboard manufacturers that sponsored rebellious street skaters. To street skating fans, Powell and the company's skaters represented the establishment. Their ties to corporate America (through sponsorship deals), seemed to support this theory. And Hawk, as the most popular member of the Bones Brigade, was heavily criticized. Skateboarder Tommy Guerrero puts it this way: "Hawk has won more contests than anyone in history, but he has also opened the door for corporate America to see what we're doing, and that changes the whole nature of things. A lot of people didn't want that door opened. For the diehards, it dilutes the whole experience." [36]

Dwindling Crowds

By 1990, street skating had overtaken vert skating in popularity. The thousands of fans that formerly flocked to vert competitions and demonstrations were disappearing. Although skateboarding's popularity had been cyclical in the past, the current decline seemed to be happening faster and more intensely than when Hawk first started skating. In his autobiography Hawk described it as a giant avalanche.

And, the decline was not limited to the United States. It was happening all over the world. Even in Japan (where Hawk and the Bones Brigades were idolized, and where their performances had attracted so many people that riot police were called in to keep order), a recent skating demonstration by team members attracted less than thirty people. The impact was felt throughout the vert skateboarding industry. Royalties from videos and board sales plummeted, sponsorships dried up, and the number of tours and competitions declined.

Despite the growing lack of interest in the sport he adored, Hawk continued competing whenever he had the opportunity. By the close of 1990, Hawk had won nearly thirty vert competitions in his lifetime. Even though he had torn cartilage under his kneecap in a demonstration in Japan, an injury that required surgery and three months off his skateboard to heal, his wins that year were impressive. Hawk won three vert contests in the United States and three in Europe, including a win in Germany that earned him the Titus Cup, a German skating award. Not surprisingly, Hawk was awarded the NSA World Championship for the seventh year in a row.

In his personal life, Hawk marked another milestone. He and Cindy were married. The wedding took place in the backyard of their Fallbrook home in front of a small group of family and friends.

Financial Woes

The newly married couple faced financial difficulties. Lack of interest in vert skating caused Hawk's income to continue to decline. And he had no savings to fall back on. Even though he had earned a great amount of money in the past, Hawk's youth and the fact that he had never expected the source of his income to dry up, led him to spend his money without thinking about the future. Hawk drove a Lexus and owned two houses. Mortgage payments on the Fallbrook house alone topped $3,000 a month. The cost of all the electronic gadgets that filled the house was also significant. Hawk loved electronic devices and bought every new product that came on the market. In fact, he proudly calls himself a "computer geek."

Hawk did not spend his money solely on himself. He was extremely generous, buying his friends and family members pricey gifts, treating them to meals at five-star restaurants, and taking them on expensive vacations.

Of his financial situation, he says:

In 1990 the industry felt the weight of rapidly declining sales and suddenly skaters weren't everywhere you looked. Skating wasn't dead—yet—but we were all worried about the future. The sport seemed to have had its day...

I was worried, because if my income shrank I would find myself in a financial hole. I had two mortgages to pay and hadn't exactly been thrifty with my money. If I wanted to go to Hawaii with my friends and they couldn't afford the tickets, I bought them. I ate at restaurants three times a day and purchased electronics like I had a disorder. New televisions—I have to buy one! New VCR—give me one! New Discman, even though I'd just bought one two months ago—I want it! During the mid 80s, I'd been known to blow

Favorite Things

In a June 2001 interview in *Sports Illustrated for Kids* and in his autobiography *Tony Hawk, Professional Skateboarder* Hawk named some of his favorite things. Here's what he said:

Favorite Sport to Watch	–	Basketball
Favorite Sport to Do	–	Skateboarding, of course!
Favorite Athlete	–	Lance Armstrong (Hawk says Armstrong, who battled cancer and now helps raise cancer awareness, inspires him.)
Favorite Animal	–	Wombat
Favorite Subject in School	–	Math
Favorite Book	–	*High Fidelity* by Nick Hornby
Favorite Movies	–	*Fast Times at Ridgemont High, The Big Lebowski*
Favorite Foods	–	Japanese food, Bagel Bites, Girl Scout Cookies, Pizza, Taco Bell
Favorite Musical Group	–	The Pixies, The Clash, AC/DC
Favorite Video Game	–	*Tony Hawk's Pro Skater 3*
Favorite Hobby	–	Producing videos
Favorite Tricks	–	Backside varial, 720, 540, backside ollie, tailgrab, 360 flip
Greatest Thrill	–	Landing a new trick for the first time

"Board Meeting," *Sports Illustrated for Kids*, June 2001.

almost a month's worth of royalties, which was anywhere from $3,000 to $5,000, at the Sharper Image [a store famous for electronic and other gadgets]. I was never too worried, because skating was still popular; it was just going through a "phase". I didn't believe it would completely die off.[37]

Unfortunately, things continued to get worse. "I learned," Hawk says, "that I can't take things for granted. It did seem like there was never going to be an end to my success, but then it dropped so suddenly that I realized I can't just take it for granted."[38]

Many of the checks Hawk received in payment for skating demonstrations bounced. Even when the checks were good, the price of gasoline, meals, and lodging often exceeded the small amount Hawk was paid. Although Hawk won the NSA world championship once again in 1991, there were only a few vert skaters left to witness it, and the prize money that used to come with the title had disappeared. Hawk also felt the pinch when the few companies that still sponsored him cut his salary. Some companies no longer offered him any cash payment, paying him in merchandise instead. Even Powell Peralta had stopped paying its skaters on the same scale as before. Royalty percentages were cut again and again.

Things got so bad that for a time Cindy's scanty earnings as a manicurist exceeded Hawk's income. In order to scrape together enough money to pay their bills, the couple put themselves on a strict budget, with Hawk getting $5 per day to pay for gasoline and fast-food meals. Says skateboarding photographer Grant Brittain, "We all remember the guy when he was destitute and eating at Taco Bell."[39]

Birdhouse Projects

Hawk was not the only one feeling the pinch; so was Powell Peralta. To cope, the company made a number of changes in the way they did business, and Hawk was becoming increasingly dissatisfied with the company. In 1991, he decided to leave Powell Peralta to start his own skateboarding company. He did not feel

Hawk's oldest son, Riley, was born in 1992. He started Birdhouse around the same time.

Female Skateboarders

When Hawk started skating professionally, there were few female skateboarders. Today this has changed, but for many years female skateboarders received less media coverage and prize money than males. There were also fewer competitions for females.

To help change this and to encourage girls to get involved in skateboarding and other action sports, a group of the world's best and most famous female skateboarders formed a group called the Action Sport's Alliance in 2005. Among this legendary group of female athletes are Vanessa Torres, Cara-Beth Burnside, Jen O'Brien, Mimi Koop, and Lyn Z. Adams Hawkins.

Since its creation the alliance has organized more competitions and demos for female skaters, including the All Girl Skate Contest. They have also raised the profile of female skaters at the X Games. Because of the alliance, since the 2006 games female skaters have received equal status in skateboarding broadcasts and competition prize money.

Anyone interested in the alliance can visit their Web site: www.actionsportsalliance.com/index.php

he was being disloyal to Peralta since he, too, was leaving the floundering company.

Starting a new skateboard company was a bold and risky step. It would take lots of money and business skills to succeed, neither of which Hawk had at the time. But he did have a vision. Hawk would recruit the hottest street and vert skateboarders to represent the company. Hawk, himself, would lead this mixed team. He thought that sponsoring both vert and street skaters would widen the appeal of the company's products and help to narrow the rift between the two skating groups.

Hawk entered into a partnership with his friend and former Powell skater, Per Werlinder, who held a college degree in business.

To help finance the company, which they named Birdhouse Projects, Hawk sold off many of his belongings.

According to writer Matt Christopher, "It was a tremendous gamble. Most new businesses fail and Hawk was dumping his life savings into skateboarding, a business that many believed was on its way out. Moreover, he had absolutely no experience in the business world. He hadn't even saved very much of the many hundred thousand dollars he had earned skating. If the business collapsed, he'd lose what little remained. But Tony Hawk had never played it safe. On many occasions he'd described his skating philosophy by saying, "I never go halfway. If I don't do my best, it eats at me. It kills me inside." He approached the business in the same way."[40]

Birdhouse was not the only new thing in Hawk's life. On December 6, 1992, he and Cindy became parents. Hawk's first son, Hudson Riley Hawk, known as Riley, was born. His birth made the risk Hawk was taking in starting Birdhouse all the more frightening. Hawk was no longer responsible just for himself and Cindy; he had a son to think about.

A Continuing Struggle

Despite Hawk and Per Werlinder's best efforts to make a success of Birdhouse, in the next few years the company did not turn a profit. Skateboarding's free-fall seemed like it would never end. Bigger, more established skateboard companies were going under. Rising costs even caused the NSA to fall apart. Things were so difficult for his family that, in 1994, Hawk was forced to sell the Fallbrook house and move his family to the house he had purchased when he was in high school.

Hawk and Per Werlinder considered closing down Birdhouse, but they hoped for an upturn in the company's fortune. In order to make ends meet, Hawk tried working as a video editor for a short time. But skateboarding was what he knew, and more importantly, what he loved. He and the Birdhouse team toured almost constantly in an effort to boost the company's profile. But interest in the team was small. "I did demos where I could count the spectators on two hands,"[41] Hawk recalls.

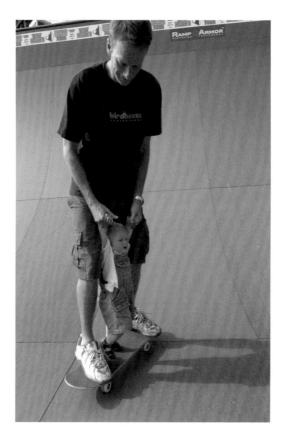

Tony introduced his sons to
skateboarding at an early age.

Under all this stress, Tony and Cindy's marriage started to unravel. Although they remained good friends, in 1994 the couple divorced, sharing joint custody of Riley. That same year, Hawk once again retired from competitive skating. It was not a difficult decision, because there were fewer and fewer vert contests to enter. The bright side was that his retirement gave him more time to devote to his son as well as to the business aspect of his company. The latter, Hawk hoped, would be just what Birdhouse needed.

Chapter 5

An X-treme Comeback

Hawk's dedication and perseverance was about to pay off. Vert skateboarding was gaining popularity in the mid-1990s. And the introduction of the X games gave the sport, and Hawk in particular, widespread exposure.

Extreme Sports

Hawk and Birdhouse continued to struggle in the early 1990s. Although it seemed like he would never earn a living as a skateboarder again, Hawk practiced everyday at the local YMCA. "Even during those dark years," he says, "I never stopped riding my skateboard and never stopped progressing as a skater."[42]

He invented at least two dozen new tricks in this time. These included a number of heel-flip tricks in which he flipped the board out from under his feet as many as three times, rotated his body, caught the board, and stuck it back under his feet before he landed. Although Hawk worked hard to master these extremely difficult maneuvers, there was so little interest in vert skating that no one took notice of his achievements. Then, in 1995, things started to look up. Hawk was asked to participate in a show called "Extreme Wheels Live."

The show featured skateboarders, BMX riders, and in-line skaters, one of whom was a young woman named Erin Lee. She and Hawk hit it off immediately and they started dating. Besides introducing the two athletes to each other, the show caught the public's interest in action sports. As a result, skateboard sales began to improve. Birdhouse decided to take advantage of the renewed public interest in vert skateboarding and reissued the Screaming Chicken Skull skateboard. To encourage sales, Hawk came out of retirement and began competing once again.

The Extreme Games

Inspired by the growing public interest in action sports, the television sports network, ESPN, launched the first Extreme Games late in 1995. The event was likened to the Olympics for action sports and became more commonly known as the X Games. The first games featured in-line skaters, BMX bikers, bungee jumpers,

Hawk was called "The Birdman" because of his high-flying tricks.

skysurfers, and street lugers, but the stars of the event were the skateboarders. And Hawk, who won the gold medal in the vert contest and the silver in street skating, became the focus of the media's attention. They called him "The Birdman" because of his high-flying stunts and ran a special feature about his life. Viewers could relate to the polite and modest man, who was not only a world-class athlete but a father and a businessman.

Although Hawk would have preferred not being singled out, once the games aired he became a star outside the skate world. He explains:

> I won the vert contest and placed second in street. The contest aired a week later, and the amount of exposure it generated was amazing. People began to recognize me on the street, in the mall, and in video stores. I'd been recognized before, but it had always been by skateboarders; now civilians came up to tell me they'd seen me on television…

> "I enjoyed skating in the contest, but I had a problem with how much attention ESPN focused on me. It was embarrassing how the spotlight seemed glued to me and ignored equally talented skaters. I met with various ESPN people and asked them to spread the exposure to include other skaters. They said there wasn't enough airtime to give every skater his due. They felt if they highlighted too many people, the viewers would get confused. Because of this my name and image became synonymous with the X Games, b ut beside skating the contest, it had nothing to do with me".[43]

Good or Bad?

Besides making Hawk a celebrity, the X Games changed the public's view of skateboarding from an outsider's pastime to a legitimate sport. But, because most people knew very little about the sport, the commentators frequently misrepresented the athletes and the sport itself. For example, the commentators created fictional rivalries between the skaters and insisted that Hawk and Andy

MacDonald, the vert silver medal winner, were hostile rivals. In reality, skateboarders are more concerned with their own individual performances than with outdoing each other. As a matter of fact, they typically cheer each other on. Hawk puts it this way: "ESPN was reporting a rivalry between Andy MacDonald and me. This couldn't be further from the truth... Andy and I were upset about it, and in every interview we did we explained that skating wasn't a sport where you had to beat somebody else. It was about having fun and outperforming yourself."[44]

This was not the only aspect of the Games that many skateboarders had problems with. The commentators frequently misidentified the different tricks and moves. Ocean Howell, a former member of the Birdhouse team, recalls his reaction:

> Most of us who were serious thought of skateboarding as an everyday activity that allowed us to make something interesting out of an alienating environment [halfpipes, or urban objects like railings]... To us it was much more an art form than a sport. But the "Extreme Games" represented skateboarding as intensively competitive, puerile [childish] thrill-seeking. Tony Hawk was considered by most skaters to be the best of all time and he was articulate and non-threatening, so ESPN focused attention on him, anointing him the "The Birdman". Looking at those bronzed, smug ESPN skateboard sportscasters, and hearing them miscall tricks, I knew this was not a world in which I could be comfortable.[45]

A Sad Passing

Despite the misgivings of skaters like Howell, as Hawk predicted, the Extreme Games helped skateboarding. The sport was suddenly very popular, as was Hawk's career and the Birdhouse Projects. At the same time, things were going well in Hawk's personal life. He and Erin were seeing more and more of each other. Not only did she make Hawk happy, she got along well with his son Riley, which pleased Hawk immensely. For the first time in years, Hawk's life seemed to be perfect. Then, tragedy struck.

Frank Hawk was diagnosed with terminal lung cancer. It was hard for Hawk to believe that his father—the man who had always been there for him—was dying. Hawk spent as much time as he could at his father's bedside. In fact, he wanted to cancel his upcoming Birdhouse tour in order to stay with his dad, but Frank would not allow it.

Hawk was skating in Pennsylvania when his father died. He recalls:

> I was skating Woodward Camp as part of a series of demos in Pennsylvania when I got a message that I had an urgent phone call. It was my mom telling me that Dad had died the night before. I didn't know what to do. I didn't start crying. There were crowds of skaters asking for autographs, but I just walked off the street course and into the woods to grieve in private. I wanted to be alone to think about what my dad had meant to me, and how much I'd miss him. It still blows me away to think of how much he did for me. I flew home that afternoon.

> We had a wake at my sister Lenore's house. People who had been involved in skating over the previous twenty years came over and exchanged affectionate stories about my dad grumbling and complaining around skate contests, but loving it at the same time. Skaters who were troublemakers told me that my dad's influence helped change their lives for the better. I knew that would have pleased my dad and meant more to him than anything else he'd done for skating.[46]

More Wins

If Frank had lived, he would have been proud of the direction that his son's career was taking. It mirrored the fortunes of the sport both men loved. Birdhouse was fast becoming the most successful skateboard manufacturer around, making Hawk a millionaire. Hawk used some of his newly found wealth to buy Erin (whom he had married in September of 1996) the house of her dreams. At the same time, Birdhouse purchased a large warehouse

Good friends Tony Hawk and Andy MacDonald compete in the vert doubles competition.

in Irvine, California, building a skating ramp inside it for Hawk and the Birdhouse team to practice on. The practice ramp was named Birdland and, although it was not in Hawk's backyard, being able to skate on it whenever he wanted made Hawk very happy. This, however, was not very often since Hawk spent most of 1996 competing and touring with the Birdhouse team.

In one contest, Hawk sprained his ankle. Two weeks later, while touring, he sprained the other one. Shortly thereafter, he reinjured the first ankle, which had never healed properly. Hawk was in constant pain and could barely walk, let alone skate. But he did not want to let down his fans, so for the next six weeks he continued to skate. An injured Hawk won the vert silver medal at the 1996 Extreme Games. His fictional rival, Andy MacDonald, won the gold.

A year later, in 1997, the two skaters switched positions and Hawk took home the gold when he performed four 540s in a row. Then, to help disprove stories about their rivalry, Hawk and MacDonald entered the vert doubles competition. The two had to skate with perfect timing in order not to slam into each other in mid-air. Their performance was flawless, earning them gold medals.

Conquering New Challenges

Hawk's continuing success made him the most famous skateboarder in the world. He was inundated with sponsorship deals, requests for public appearances, media interviews, and autograph-signing sessions. Arranging his schedule became a difficult juggling act. Hawk hired his sister Pat as his manager. With Pat handling the details, he hoped he would have more time to skate. Despite his celebrity status, Hawk's goals had not changed. Learning new tricks and improving as a skater were his top priorities. "My job description is professional skateboarder," Hawk told *EXPN* magazine in 2007. "It's what I love doing, and that's what drives me. I do everything else because it allows me to skate."[47]

In 1998, Hawk got a chance to skate in a Birdhouse video. It was called *The End*, because at thirty years old, Hawk was anticipating the end of his skating career. The film showcased the incredible skating skill of each member of the Birdhouse team. For his part, Hawk wanted to land the three tricks that he had been practicing for years but had not yet been able to perform, a varial 720, a 900, and a loop. The first is a stunt in which the skater spins the board in a full circle without using his hands while performing a 720. The second is an almost impossible feat

With his passion and dedication, Hawk became the most famous skateboarder in the world.

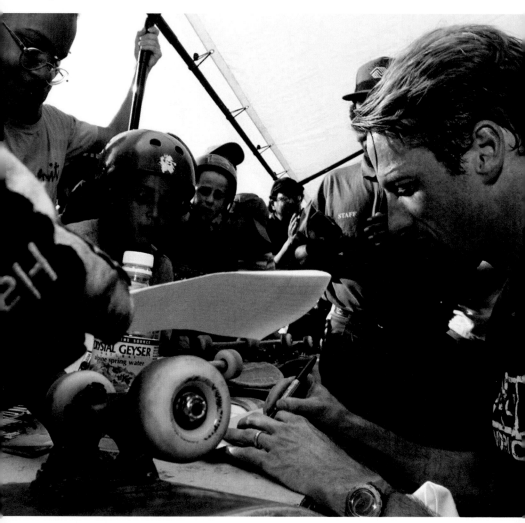

in which the skater completes five full rotations. The last involves skating around a 360-degree loop.

In his past attempts at the varial 720 and the 900, Hawk could never get enough height to successfully complete the stunts. In an attempt to solve this problem, Birdhouse had a huge two-story-high skate ramp built in a bullfighting arena in Tijuana,

A Model for Tarzan

Hawk's performance in the video *The End* was used as a model for the Disney animated movie, *Tarzan*. The main animator for *Tarzan* watched *The End* with his skateboarding son. Before seeing the skateboarding video, the animator was having trouble trying to depict Tarzan's body movements. Seeing Hawk's movements inspired him. He animated Hawk's movements as he skated the ramp and the loop. These sequences became the basis for Tarzan's movements as he swung from tree to tree in the jungle. In fact, many of the cartoon character's moves are exact copies of Hawk's.

Hawk, whose son Riley was a huge Disney fan, was glad to help the company, and felt honored to be part of the movie. Disney interviewed Hawk for a documentary about the animated movie and invited him to the premiere. Although Hawk was already a celebrity in his own right, the modest man spent much of his time at the event trying to get his picture taken with the actresses and actors who served as the voices of the animated characters.

The lead animator of the Disney movie, Tarzan, used Hawk's movements during the ramp and loop as a model for Tarzan's.

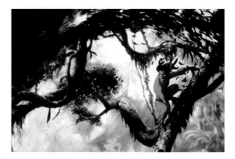

Mexico. A giant circular loop was connected to the ramp. At first, skating the massive ramp was frightening. Its size caused Hawk to gather so much speed that he was afraid of slamming into the sides. But once he got used to it, he liked the way it allowed him to soar high into the air. He describes what it was like:

> If I normally went six feet [1.83m] high on airs, I went ten [3.05m]. I could do twelve-foot-high [3.66m] 540s and go fourteen feet [4.27m] on Japanese airs, one of my favorite airs. To do one, you have to do a backside air, but when you grab around your front foot to pull your board back you tweak it. I had some problems at first, because I'd hang in the air so long I wouldn't arc like a normal air; I'd shoot up and feel like I was plummeting straight down. But it was fun.[48]

After four days, Hawk landed the varial 720. The 900, however, continued to challenge him. The loop was a different kind of stunt. Skating a complete circle defied gravity. Indeed, in the future, Hawk would compare the feeling he got while skating the loop to riding in a roller coaster and he would admit that he could not tell when he was upside down. But Hawk was sure he could do it, and he did. "I never doubted that it could be done, so I kept trying until I figured out how to pump all the way through,"[49] he says.

The 900

The demands on Hawk's time continued to increase. In March 1999, his second son, Spencer, was born. Tony wanted to spend more time with his growing family, which was difficult with his competition schedule. He felt satisfied with all he had achieved. And, although he wanted to keep skating, he decided that he would retire from competitions at the end of the year. But before he could do so, there was still one thing he wanted to do—land the 900. There was no better place to try it than at the X Games.

Hawk's performance in the vert portion of the games that year was not convincing, winning him the bronze medal. He entered a new event, best trick, in which each skater had twenty minutes

Hawk performed at the 1999 X Games, winning the Skateboard Vert Best Trick event when he nailed the varial 720 and the 900.

to perform. Hawk landed a varial 720 right away, then decided to go for the 900. Over and over, he spun in the air then slammed hard into the ramp. "I was going to make it or be carried off the ramp on a stretcher,"[50] he confesses.

A Long Road

For Tony Hawk, landing the 900 at the 1999 X Games was the culmination of years of practice. The first time he tried the trick was in 1986, while he was teaching at a skating camp in France. He could not get high enough or spin fast enough to come close to landing it and stopped trying for almost a decade.

In 1996, Hawk tried the trick again. On his third rotation, he lost track of where he was. His board flew into the audience and he slammed into the ramp bloodying his shins. Later that year, he broke a rib in another attempt.

He continued to try to land the 900 for the next four years. Because the damage to his body was so great, he did not practice continuously. In his autobiography, he likened the effects of the stunt to being in a car crash. At one point, he hurt his back so badly he could barely walk. Yet mastering the stunt never left his thoughts. When the time was right, he was sure that he would land it.

He was so focused on his goal that he was completely unaware that his twenty minutes were up. Neither the pain he was inflicting on his body, nor the roar of the cheering crowd affected him. Each failed attempt taught him something new, bringing him closer to his goal. After eleven grueling failures, Tony finally nailed the 900! When he landed on the ramp, he was so surprised that it took him a moment to understand that he had realized his dream. Once he comprehended what he had done, he raised his fists in the air in a sign of victory. "I just felt this great sense of relief that I'd finally conquered this beast that had plagued me for so long,"[51] he recalls.

With that, the crowd erupted into wild cheering. The other skaters swarmed onto the ramp to congratulate him. "This is the best day of my life,"[52] Hawk screamed.

Hawk had made skateboarding history. Landing the 900 guaranteed his legacy as one of the world's all-time great athletes. But it was his resolve to achieve a seemingly impossible goal that amazed and inspired skaters and nonskaters alike. Because of his unflagging determination and persistence on that day in 1999, Tony Hawk became a living legend.

Chapter 6

Still Going Strong

Hawk's retirement did not remove him from the public eye. If anything, his schedule was busier than ever, making him a skateboarding icon. "It was as if I hit the gas pedal, when I was aiming for the brake." [53] he jokes.

Still Skating

Although officially retired, Hawk did not stop competing entirely. He continued to enter the X Games, winning the gold medal with Andy Macdonald in vert doubles every year through 2002. He continued to tour extensively, but, in an effort to spend more time

Even in retirement, Hawk continued to enter the X Games.

Tony tried to spend as much time with Erin, Riley, and Spencer as he could.

with his family, he became more selective about the events he took part in. Still, he spent a lot of time on the road. He describes what this was like:

Life on the road is a world unto itself. There is no way to describe the reality of being in a different city every day, sleeping in a new bed every night, and sharing the close company of a few others along the way.

It is in turn exciting, grueling, glamorous, disgusting, tiring, comical, stressful, and shocking—but it is never boring. As a husband and father… I find touring all the more surreal. My life shifts from normal spousal duties at home—like fixing breakfast for the kids, taking them to school, attending parent-teacher conferences, taking out the trash, paying bills, waiting on line at the DMV, reading *Hop on Pop*, and watching *Sponge Bob Square Pants*—to flying in private jets, performing in front of thousands of people, getting VIP treatment at restaurants and clubs, and having everything paid for by someone else. Neither lifestyle allows sufficient sleep, but I am completely thankful to have both…. Striking a healthy balance between being home and being away is the biggest challenge of my life. I've become selective about which events or projects I get involved in.[54]

Promoting the Sport

When he was not touring or spending time with his family (which grew in 2001 when his third son, Keegan, was born), Hawk worked hard to ensure that skateboarding remained a popular and respected sport. He also continued to promote the Tony Hawk brand. He gave his name to a line of clothing, athletic shoes, skateboards, and skateboarding-related toys, as well as a chain of Hawk Skate stores. Together these enterprises earned an estimated $300 million a year, $10 million of which went to Hawk annually. He also served as the spokesperson for a variety of products, including skateboard trucks and helmets, sunglasses,

From shoes to toys, Hawk endorses skateboarding-related products.

and various foods. Hawk's association with a product practically guaranteed a jump in sales. Says fellow skateboarder Bucky Lasek, "The guy is golden... He could put his name on toilet paper and sell it to the world."[55]

Although he was offered hundreds of marketing deals of this kind, Hawk refused to promote a product unless he believed in it and his involvement would help to promote skateboarding. "It's about keeping true to what I do and to the sport ... instead of just making a quick buck,"[56] he insists.

Tony Hawk's Pro Skater

When Activision approached Hawk about developing a video game named *Tony Hawk's Pro Skater,* he was thrilled. A project of this kind would combine two of his favorite activities: skateboarding and video gaming. Always a perfectionist, Hawk insisted that the game be an accurate representation of skateboarding. "I played video games since *Missile Command* at the local arcade. When I got a chance to work on a game, I wanted it right,"[57] he says.

To ensure that this would be so, Hawk monitored every step of the game's development. For instance, he insisted that all the skating maneuvers shown in the game were realistic. To make sure this was so, according to skateboarder Ocean Howell, "Activision paid pros to skate in full-body sensor suits, digitally mapping every microscopic gesture of a skater's style: how far down he crouches before doing a trick, whether his elbow is bent or straight at the peak of the trick, how close together his feet are when he lands."[58]

This was just the beginning of Hawk's involvement. As the designers worked on the game, they sent updated versions to him so that he could provide feedback on how to improve the product. With Hawk's approval, the game hit the stores in the fall of 1999. It was an unprecedented success. Tony describes what happened:

I thought I'd make a little bit of money off the game, but mostly I was amped to help create a good skating game. There was no way I thought it would take off beyond the skate world, but almost immediately it sold out in toy

The popularity of the video game Tony Hawk's Pro Skater went far beyond skating enthusiasts.

stores…. Video game magazines put me on their covers, and I can't remember anything but stellar reviews (this has more to do with the game designers than with me though!) In a matter of months … *Pro Skater* was the best selling PlayStation game of the 1999 Christmas Season. "The thing that I love about the game is that it's the perfect marriage between the mainstream and the skateboarding scene. Skaters love the game, and people who would never go near a board rave about it. It bridged a gap between hardcore skaters and mainstream viewers.[59]

Since then, Tony Hawk skateboard games have been released every year. The series, which has won three Blockbuster video game awards, has become one of the best-selling video-game franchises ever. It earns Hawk an estimated $6 million annually. Not only that, the games introduced Hawk and skateboarding to a whole new audience. "There are so many kids who started playing my video game who had never skated in their lives and then they thought it looked cool," Hawk explains, "so they went out and bought a board and tried it. And they liked it."[60]

Boom Boom Huck Jam

Hawk put in just as much time and effort when he launched his extreme sport touring megashow, the Boom Boom Huck Jam in 2002. It features the world's best motorcross riders, BMX bikers, and skateboarders doing their most daring tricks accompanied by live rock, heavy metal, and punk bands. Hawk explains, "I just was doing a lot of exhibitions in recent years, seeing the crowds grow and grow. And for the most part, all of our exhibitions were sideshows to bigger events, be it concert tours or state fairs or football half-time shows. I felt like there was enough interest where we could be the focus of the tour."[61]

Although Hawk believed in his vision, he could not get sponsorship for the show. So, just as with Birdhouse Projects, he took a big risk, laying out over $1 million of his own money to make his vision a reality. The money was needed to build a system of huge portable ramps used in the tour, as well as to pay for the lighting, transportation, crew, and athletes. Besides Hawk, other people involved in the project included Andy MacDonald, Bob Burnquist, and Shaun White on skateboards, BMXers Dave Mirra and Dennis McCoy, and freestyle motorcross bikers Ronnie Faist and Carey Hart, to name just a few. "The goal," Hawk explained before the debut of the first show, "is to build something that will live beyond my involvement in it. This first show is either going to be a huge success or the most expensive party I've ever thrown for a bunch of my friends." [62]

Boom Boom Huck Jam featured extreme sports athletes along with live music.

Saying Thanks

Tony Hawk has won many awards in his lifetime, including the ESPN 2001 Lifetime Achievement Award. When he received the ESPN award, he had a chance to recognize all the important people in his life, and pay tribute to his father.

Here is a an excerpt from his acceptance speech: "I would first like to thank ESPN for giving skateboarding so much recognition and support over the recent years, and for giving us a medium to display our talents. On a personal level, I wish to thank everyone that has believed in me over the years—my ever supportive family (Mom, Steve, Pat, Lenore), my beautiful wife...(Erin), my sons Riley and Spencer. Everyone at Birdhouse... Stacy Peralta and the... Brigade. I would also like to thank the fans of skateboarding everywhere, but thanks most of all to my father, who could never have imagined that driving his son to the skate park every day would amount to this. This one is for you dad."

Tony Hawk. *Between Boardslides and Burnout*

Hawk received the ESPN Lifetime Achievement Award in 2001.

Hawk's financial gamble paid off. The Boom Boom Huck Jam proved to be an even bigger success than Hawk imagined. Says skater and Huck Jam performer Bob Burnquist: "Somebody needed to think of the next feasible step. That's what Hawk has done. With his business sense, it's no surprise that he is the one."[63]

According to Hawk, the show got its name because, "We 'huck' ourselves into the air throughout the show, and it is a 'jam', not a competition. Sometimes we fall down and go 'boom.'"[64] The oddly titled event has proven to be the most successful action sports show of all time. Since its debut in 2002, it has been presented in arenas and Six Flag parks throughout North America.

Writer Hampton Sides attended the first Boom Boom Huck Jam at the Mandalay Bay Arena in Las Vegas, and describes the start of the show in this way. "The house lights go out and a bevy of… young models in silver lame body stockings, white Lone Ranger masks, and platinum-blond wigs come out holding signs that signal the start of the HuckJam. From the stage, swaddled in a dry-ice haze, the punk band Social Distortion cranks up.

"Here come the skateboarders—zipping down, one by one, from a 30-foot-high [9.14m] perch in the scaffolding. Like buzzy, looping electrons, Bob Burnquist, Andy Macdonald, Lincoln Ueda, Bucky Lasek, and Shaun White—five of the preeminent vert skaters in the world—power through the massive bronze bowl of the halfpipe and launch high over the lip in a dervish of spins and kickflips, ollies and McTwists. And then—the man we've all been waiting for dives down the ramp, lanky and tough-sinewed and—true to his name—curiously avian [birdlike], with a beaky nose and flailing arms and big, alert eyes. He soars through the air and lands effortlessly on the platform with the other skaters, Quetzalcoatl among mere mortals: *The Birdman*. "Calmly drinking in the adulation, Hawk hoists his board over his helmeted head and tips it toward the roaring crowd … as if to say "Welcome."[65]

Doing His Part

With the success of the Boom Boom Huck Jam, Hawk became richer than he ever dreamed. Although Hawk enjoyed the comforts and luxuries that wealth brought him, he would always be first and foremost a skater. "I just set out to keep skating and keep getting better. So anything else, in terms of fame or finances or opportunity is incidental,"[66] he says.

In an effort to help others experience the joy of skating, in 2002 Hawk started the Tony Hawk Foundation. Its primary function is to help communities raise money to build public skateparks. Having grown up feeling like an outsider because he did not do traditional sports or conform to social pressure, Hawk wanted to extend the sport's popularity and make skating facilities accessible to everyone. In fact, he currently donates his demo fees to the foundation.

According to an article on the Tony Hawk Foundation's Web site,

> After receiving thousands of emails from parents and children across America who either did not have a safe, legal place to skate or were ostracized—and in some cases arrested—for skating on public property, Hawk decided to establish a foundation with the mission of serving this population. He wanted to help them develop quality places to practice the sport that gives them much-needed exercise and a sense of self-esteem…

> Since its inception, the Tony Hawk Foundation has sought to foster lasting improvements in society, with an emphasis on serving underprivileged children. Through grants and other charitable donations, the foundation supports programs focused on the creation of public skateboard parks.

> For Tony Hawk, skateboarding was a healthy outlet and a recreational challenge, and it provided a social group of creative, like-minded individuals. It was also a sport that helped him build confidence, taught him to persevere, and through his mentoring of younger skaters helped him develop leadership skills. The Tony Hawk Foundation works every day to be able to bring these same lessons to children across the country.[67]

Stand Up for Skateparks

One way the Tony Hawk Foundation raises money is through an annual benefit called Stand Up for Skateparks. Held in Beverly Hills, the benefit is chaired by a diverse group including such famous people as Hawk, Sean Penn, Stacy Peralta, David Spade, Shaun White, and Jamie Lee Curtis. The benefit features live music and a demo by Hawk and other action sports stars such as Shaun White, Bucky Lasek, and Mat Hoffman. After the demo, the guests, who include many celebrities, get to bid on a wide range of unique items in a silent auction. In 2006, two of the most interesting items were a brand new Jeep that had been customized to represent Tony Hawk, and a chance to be a character in a new Tony Hawk video game.

Since it was created, the fundraiser has been a huge success. In 2006, the event raised $950,000. Hawk hopes that future events will be even more successful.

The Aims of the Foundation

The foundation, which requires skaters work with government officials to plan parks, is doing just that and more. In its first three years, it raised $1.3 million to build 291 skateparks in large and small communities throughout the United States. Waldport, Oregon, is one such community. Resident Scott Beckstead explains what the foundation has done for the young people there: "Prior to the skatepark, no one was doing anything for the kids. But now even the youth center has been revitalized. The skatepark is a symbol to the kids that the City cares about them. The kids have learned that what you say and do does matter, and hard work will pay off. They realize they can make a difference."[68]

In fact, the foundation has been so successful that Hawk has reached out to other foundations. In April 2007, he (along with eleven other famous athletes) formed the Athletes for

Six Flags is creating a roller coaster based on Hawk's skating tricks.

Hope Foundation, a group that aims to link together charitable organizations run by athletes. It is Hawk's hope that through all his work in these organizations, he can share some of his good fortune with others.

A Fitting Farewell

In 2003, Hawk took time away from his busy schedule to appear in the X Games one last time. As a fitting end to his competitive career, he once again nailed the 900 and received the gold medal in the best trick competition. At that time, he was still the only skater in the world to have mastered the difficult stunt. Once again, he told the world that his days of competitive skating were over. This time Hawk's retirement would be his last.

Once again, Hawk pledged to spend more time with his wife and family. But it was too late. All the time he spent touring and managing his many business and charitable ventures had taken a heavy toll on his marriage. He and Erin were divorced in 2004. Two years later, he married Lhotse Merriam, a lingerie designer, on a heart-shaped island in Fiji.

Still Going Strong

Not competing has not slowed Hawk down. Today, he is still going strong. If anything, he is more popular than ever. As a middle-aged father of three, he does not fit the image of the type of person young people relate to. But his youthful attitude, his genuine devotion to skating, and his extraordinary achievements have made him an idol for young people everywhere and a role model that parents appreciate.

Besides running his foundation and a multimillion dollar business empire with his sharp business skills, he appears in movies and television programs, works as a sports commentator, is a frequent presenter and winner at awards shows, and is the author of three books about his life, one of which was a bestseller. His fame is so great that a Six Flags amusement park is building a roller coaster based on his skating tricks. Despite all his success and the constant demands on his time, skateboarding remains his great passion. The man who invented more than eighty different skateboarding tricks still skates at least two hours a day and has no intention of quitting. "I can't believe after all this time my main job is still riding a skateboard," he confesses. "The lean times taught me to never take advantage of it. I am having a blast, and I am incredibly thankful."[69]

Notes

Introduction: Ups and Downs

1. Tony Hawk, NPR.org, "Do What You Love," All Things Considered, 7/24/06, www.npr.org/templates/story/story.php?storyId=5568583.
2. Tony Hawk, NPR.org, "Do What You Love".
3. David G. Teen Ink, "The Real Tony Hawk" www.teenink.com/Past/2003/October/17034.html.
4. Tony Hawk, NPR.org, "Do What You Love".
5. Jean-Jacques Taylor, Dallas Morning News.com, "Hawk Soars Far Above His Sport," 10/27/06, www.dallasnews.com/sharedcontent/dws/spt/columnists/jtaylor/stories/102806dnspotaylor.2c95f91.html.
6. Tony Hawk, *Between Boardslides and Burnout*. New York: Regan Books, 2002. p. 10.
7. Tony Hawk, *Between Boardslides and Burnout*. p. 2.

Chapter 1: A Perfect Match

8. Tony Hawk with Sean Mortimer, *Hawk: Occupation Skateboarder*. New York: Regan Books, 2001. p. 8.
9. Tony Hawk with Sean Mortimer, *Hawk: Occupation Skateboarder*. p. 11.
10. Tony Hawk with Sean Mortimer, *Tony Hawk Professional Skateboarder*. New York: Regan Books, 2002. p. 8.
11. Tony Hawk with Sean Mortimer, *Tony Hawk Professional Skateboarder*. p. 14.
12. Tony Hawk with Sean Mortimer, *Hawk: Occupation Skateboarder*. p. 19.
13. Tony Hawk with Sean Mortimer, *Hawk: Occupation Skateboarder*. p. 26.
14. Tony Hawk with Sean Mortimer, *Tony Hawk Professional Skateboarder*. p. 27.
15. Quoted in Denise Henry, "Tony Hawk," *Scholastic Action*. 2/28/05, p. 4.

Chapter 2: Developing a New Style

16. Tony Hawk with Sean Mortimer, *Hawk: Occupation Skateboarder*. p. 40.
17. Tony Hawk with Sean Mortimer, *Tony Hawk Professional Skateboarder*. p. 62.
18. Tony Hawk, NPR.org, "Do What You Love,".
19. Quoted in "Hawk-Eye-View," *Scholastic Choices*, November/December 2002, p. 5.
20. Tony Hawk with Sean Mortimer, *Hawk: Occupation Skateboarder*. p. 34.
21. Quoted in Lee Crane, TransWorld Skateboarding, "Tony Hawk in the New Yorker," 7/23/99 www.skateboarding.com/skate/stories/article/0,23271,201319,00.html.
22. Quoted in Hampton Sides, Outside Online, "Birdman Drops In," October 2002, www.outside.away.com/outside/news/200210/200210_birdman_drops_4adp.
23. Tony Hawk with Sean Mortimer, *Hawk: Occupation Skateboarder*. p. 40.
24. Tony Hawk with Sean Mortimer, *Tony Hawk Professional Skateboarder*. p. 54.

Chapter 3: Riding the Wave

25. Tony Hawk with Sean Mortimer, *Tony Hawk Professional Skateboarder*. p. 75.
26. Tony Hawk with Sean Mortimer, *Tony Hawk Professional Skateboarder*. p. 73.
27. Tony Hawk with Sean Mortimer, *Tony Hawk Professional Skateboarder*. p. 76.
28. Quoted in Hampton Sides, Outside Online, "Birdman Drops In,".
29. Quoted in Tony Hawk.com, Q and A, www.tonyhawk.com/qanda_apr_jun_04.cfm.
30. Tony Hawk with Sean Mortimer, *Tony Hawk Professional Skateboarder*. p. 83.
31. Quoted in Tony Hawk with Sean Mortimer, *Hawk: Occupation Skateboarder*. p. 134.

Chapter 4: Barely Getting By

32. Quoted in Tony Hawk with Sean Mortimer, *Hawk: Occupation Skateboarder*. p. 138.
33. Matt Christopher, *On the Halfpipe with Tony Hawk*. NY: Little Brown and Company, 2001. p. 51.
34. Tony Hawk with Sean Mortimer, *Hawk: Occupation Skateboarder*. p. 154.
35. Quoted in "Board Meeting," *Sports Illustrated for Kids*, June 2001, p. 29–37. http://web.ebscohost.com/ehost/delivery/vid=58&hid=21&sid=6024bad7-164c-4028-af65.
36. Quoted in Tim Layden, "Making Millions," *Sports Illustrated*, 6/10/02, p. 80–89. http://web.ebscohost.com/ehost/delivery/vid=51&hid=21&sid=6024bad7-164c-4028-af65.
37. Tony Hawk with Sean Mortimer, *Hawk: Occupation Skateboarder*. p. 160.
38. Quoted in Jeff H., Jiadai L., David G., Teen Ink, "Skateboarder Tony Hawk, October 2003, www.teenink.com/Past/2003/October/17025.html.
39. Quoted in Hampton Sides, Outside Online, "Birdman Drops In,".
40. Matt Christopher, *On the Halfpipe with Tony Hawk*. p. 60.
41. Quoted in Tim Layden, "Making Millions,".

Chapter 5: An X-treme Comeback

42. Tony Hawk, NPR.org, "Do What You Love".
43. Tony Hawk with Sean Mortimer, *Hawk: Occupation Skateboarder*. p. 190.
44. Tony Hawk with Sean Mortimer, *Tony Hawk Professional Skateboarder*. p. 130.
45. Ocean Howell, Topic Magazine, "Extreme Market Research," 2003. www.webdelsol.com/Topic/articles/o4/images/howell.html.
46. Tony Hawk with Sean Mortimer, *Tony Hawk Professional Skateboarder*. p. 123–124.
47. Quoted in Micah Abrams, EXPN.com, "Just Don't Call Him Retired," March 28, 2007, www.expn.go.com/expn/story?pageName=maghawk.

48. Tony Hawk with Sean Mortimer, *Hawk: Occupation Skateboarder*. p. 214.
49. Quoted in Tony Hawk.com, "Q and A," www.tonyhawk.com/qanda_oct_dec_02.cfm.
50. "Flyboy," *People*, January 8, 2001, p. 21.
51. Quoted in CBS News, 60 Minutes II, "Tony Hawk Takes Off," June 16, 2004, www.cbsnews.com/stories/2002/12/10/60II/main532506.shtml.
52. Quoted in Hampton Sides, Outside Online, "Birdman Drops In,".

Chapter 6: Still Going Strong

53. Tony Hawk with Sean Mortimer, *Hawk: Occupation Skateboarder*. p. 259.
54. Tony Hawk, *Between Boardslides and Burnout*. p. 1.
55. Quoted in Tim Layden, "Making Millions,".
56. Quoted in Jeff H., Jiadai L., David G., Teen Ink, "Skateboarder Tony Hawk".
57. Quoted in Mark Hyman, "How Tony Hawk Stays Aloft," *Business Week*, November 13, 2006, p. 84–88. htttp://web.ebscohost.com/ehost/detail?vid=7&hid=19&sid=df982507-1b25-4abe-886d-079a....
58. Ocean Howell, Topic Magazine, "Extreme Market Research".
59. Tony Hawk with Sean Mortimer, Hawk: *Occupation Skateboarder*. p. 247.
60. Quoted in Tim Layden, "Making Millions,".
61. Quoted in CBS News, 60 Minutes II, "Tony Hawk Takes Off,".
62. Quoted in Tim Layden, "Making Millions,".
63. Quoted in Tim Layden, "Making Millions,".
64. Quoted in "Losers Turn Legit Thanks to Legendary Hawk," *Toronto Star*, July 25, 2005, htttp://web.ebscohost.com/ehost/delivery?vid=22&hid=21&sid=6024bad7-164c-4028-af65...
65. Hampton Sides, Outside Online, "Birdman Drops In".
66. Quoted in "Losers Turn Legit Thanks to Legendary Hawk".

67. Tony Hawk Foundation, "Background," www.tonyhawkfoundation.org/background.asp.
68. Quoted on Tony Hawk Foundation, "Success Stories," www.tonyhawkfoundation.org/success_stories.asp.
69. Quoted Xavier Tobias Jones, "Chairman of the Board: Tony Hawk Q&A," *Fort Worth Star Telegram*, October 27, 2006, p.D13.

1968

Anthony Frank Hawk is born on May 12, 1968.

1979

Hawk is sponsored by Dogtown.

1980

Hawk joins the Bones Brigade.

1983

Hawk turns pro. He places 3rd in Rusty Harris Pro, his first pro competition. He wins Del Mar, St. Petersburg Pro, and Spring Nationals Pro competitions. His father starts the NSA. The Screaming Chicken Skull skateboard is released. He is named NSA World Champion.

1984

Hawk meets Cindy Dunbar. He wins Booney Ramp Bang, Sundeck Eastern Pro, Summer Series Halfpipe and Pool Finals competitions. He is named NSA World Champion.

1985

Hawk wins Del Mar, the Badlands, King of the Mount, Arkansas Ramp Jam, and Shut up and Skate competitions. He is named NSA World Champion.

1986

Hawk buys his first house. He graduates from high school.

He wins Transworld Skateboard Championship, Holiday Havoc, Festival of Sports, Chicago Blowout, and Southern Shred competitions. He is named NSA World Champion.

1987

Hawk wins Southeast, Skate Wave, V.P. Fair competitions. He is named NSA World Champion.

1988

He wins Skate Fest, Capital Burnout, Gotta Grind, Ramp Riot, and Heartland Invasion competitions. He is named NSA World Champion. He retires for the first time. He buys the Fallbrook home and builds a giant ramp.

1989

Hawk comes out of retirement. He wins Scandinavian Open and Street, Titus Cup and Street, St. Pete Showdown and Street competitions. He is named NSA World Champion.

1990

Hawk marries Cindy Dunbar. He wins Del Mar Fair and San Francisco Street Competition. He is named NSA World Champion.

1991

Hawk wins Norfolk, Powell Street, Kona, France, Capital Burnout, Monster Ramp Jam, and Shut Up and Skate competitions. He is named NSA World Champion.

1992

Hawk leaves Powell Peralta and starts Birdhouse Projects. His son Riley is born. He wins NSA Finals and Street.

1993

Hawk wins Munster Ramp Vert and Street and Belgium competitions.

1995

Hawk and Cindy Dunbar divorce. He wins Hard Rock World Championship, and Extreme Games vert. The media names him The Birdman. He meets Erin Lee. His father dies.

1996

Hawk and Erin Lee marry. He wins Hard Rock Triple Crown, and Destination Extreme competitions.

1997

Hawk wins X Games vert and doubles, London, and Hard Rock World Championship.

1998

Hawk wins X Games doubles, SPOT, B3, Triple Crown, Goodwill Games, and Hard Rock World Championship. He fails to do a 900 in his video, *The End*. He skates a loop.

1999

Hawk performs the 900 at the X Games. He wins the X Games doubles. His son Spencer is born. *Tony Hawk Pro Skater* video game is released. He retires again.

2000

Hawk's autobiography, *Hawk: Occupation Skateboarder*, is published.

2001

Hawk's son Keegan is born.

2002

Hawk launches the Tony Hawk Foundation. His autobiography, *Tony Hawk Professional Skateboarder* and his book *Between Boardslides and Burnout* are published.

2003

Hawk does a 900 at the X Games and wins first place. He retires for the last time.

2004

Hawk and Erin Lee divorce.

2006

Hawk marries Lhotse Merriam.

For More Information

Books

Michael Brooke, *The Concrete Wave*. Toronto: Warwick Publishing, 1999. Traces the history of skateboarding with an interview with Tony Hawk.

Tony Hawk, Sean Mortimer, *Tony Hawk Professional Skateboarder*. New York: Regan Books, 2002. A short version of Tony's autobiography (with photographs). Suitable for young adults.

Raymond Miller, *Star of Sports*—Tony Hawk. San Diego: Kidhaven Press, 2004. A short biography.

Todd Peterson, *Tony Hawk Skateboarder and Businessman*. NY: Facts on File, 2005. A young adult book biography.

Periodicals

Karen Barrow, "Fly like a Hawk," *Scholastic SuperScience*, May 2005.

"Board Meeting," *Sports Illustrated for Kids*, June 2001.

Christian Hosoi, "Tony Hawk Interview," *Juice Magazine*, Issue 58, December 2006.

Tim Layden, "Making Millions," *Sports Illustrated*, June 10, 2002.

DVDs

The Bones Brigade Video Show. Santa Barbara, Cal.: Powell Peralta, 1984.

The End. San Diego, Cal.: Birdhouse Projects, 2000.

The Search for Animal Chin Special Edition. Santa Barbara, Cal.: Powell Peralta, 2005.

Ultimate X: The Movie, Burbank, Cal: Walt Disney Videos, 2003.

Web Sites

About.com "Skateboarding" (www.skateboard.about.com/). Lots of information about every aspect of skateboarding.

Board Crazy Skateboarding (www.board-crazy.co.uk/). Information about skateboarding, including a detailed "tricktionary" in which skating tricks are described.

Exploratorium, "Skateboard Science" (www.exploratorium. edu/skateboarding/). Interesting site that describes the physics of skateboarding. Includes a webcast and glossary.

Skateboard.com (www.skateboard.com/). Comprehensive information about every aspect of skateboarding.

Tony Hawk (www.tonyhawk.com/). Tony Hawk's official Web site includes a biography, a trick timeline, videos and pictures, and a question and answer section in which Tony answers fans' e-mail.

Tony Hawk Foundation (www.tonyhawkfoundation.org/). Lots of information about the foundation and how to get money to build a skate park.

TransWorld Skateboarding (www.skateboarding.com/skate/). The Web site for this skateboarding magazine.

Barbara Sheen is the author of more than forty books for young people. She lives in New Mexico with her family. In her spare time she likes to swim, walk, garden, and cook. Although she is too old to skateboard, she thinks Tony Hawk is cool!